EVERYONE IS TALKING ABOUT

The Silent Passage

"Menopause. In our youth-obsessed culture, the very word is a room-emptier: The pregnancy club is for women a joyous one—the menopause club is one nobody wants to admit she has joined. . . . Gail Sheehy has broken the taboo. She has got notable women talking on the record about the subject. And she has led the way, with candor about herself. . . ."

—Tina Brown,
in her editorial comment
on Sheehy's article in *Vanity Fair*

"It is probably the least discussed of the major M words in women's lives. . . . Now Sheehy, fifty-four, has set out to end the shame—and the ignorance that fosters it. Her new book, THE SILENT PASSAGE: MENOPAUSE is based on interviews with dozens of medical experts and more than one hundred American women across the socioeconomic spectrum. It offers information on hormone-replacement therapy . . . and urges the millions of baby boomers . . . to view the change as 'the gateway to a second adulthood' rather than a harbinger of the end."

—Kim Hubbard, *People*

"The information is welcome, and Sheehy deserves a cheer for laying on the line what your doctor, your mother and your best friend won't tell you. . . ."

—Amanda Heller, *Boston Sunday Globe*

The Silent Passage

menopause

~

Gail Sheehy

POCKET BOOKS

New York   London   Toronto   Sydney   Tokyo   Singapore

The author of this book is not a physician and the ideas, procedures, and suggestions in this book are not intended as a substitute for the medical advice of a trained health professional. All matters regarding your health require medical supervision. Consult your physician before adopting the suggestions in this book, as well as about any condition that may require diagnosis or medical attention. The author and publisher disclaim any liability arising directly or indirectly from the use of the book.

POCKET BOOKS, a division of Simon & Schuster Inc.
1230 Avenue of the Americas, New York, NY 10020

Copyright © 1991, 1992, 1993, 1995 by G. Merritt Corporation

Published by arrangement with Random House, Inc.

ISBN: 0-671-79931-2

First Pocket Books printing May 1993

20   19   18   17   16   15   14   13   12   11   10

POCKET and colophon are registered trademarks of Simon & Schuster Inc.

Cover photo by Carin Riley

Printed in the U.S.A.

Contents

~

Contents

The Perimenopause Panic

The Menopause Gateway

Contents

Coalescence

Introduction

~

When *The Silent Passage* was first published in America, in May 1992, it touched a nerve much deeper than I had imagined. From my explorations in America, Canada, and Europe I had some inkling of how backward we are in basic scientific research on a condition that goes back to prehistory. Menopause is not some new environmental toxin, after all. When Dr. Bernadine Healy became the first woman director of the U.S. National Institutes of Health (NIH) in 1991, she summed up the state of our knowledge on the subject: "It's disgraceful that in our sophisticated world of medicine, with our phenomenal track record, we still can't answer simple questions about menopause." But I had no concept of the shocking breadth of fear, shame, and denial that women would discover among themselves. Nor did they.

Even a woman as strong and resilient as Barbara Bush finally realized why, when she hit fifty, she had flirted with the idea of suicide. "I was very severely depressed," she writes in her memoir. "I hid it from everyone, including my closest friends . . . I felt ashamed." Like so many women of her World War II generation, she kept silent. "My 'code' told me that you should not think about self, but others," she writes. "And yet, there I was, wallowing in self-pity. I knew it was wrong, but I couldn't seem to pull out of it." She never mentioned the M word. She never even associated hormonal changes with her dismal moods.

"Night after night George held me weeping in his arms while I tried to explain my feelings. I almost wonder why he didn't leave me." Her husband's suggestion that she see a psychiatrist only drove her deeper into gloom. Alone in the pit of menopausal malaise, she admits, she sometimes had to pull her car off the highway to stop herself from deliberately crashing into a tree or an oncoming vehicle.

Only today, almost twenty years after the fact, is Barbara Bush able to give that brief torment a name: "It seems so simple to me now: I was just the right age, fifty-one years old, for menopause."

A generation and a half after Mrs. Bush's experience, we were still just as ignorant. I went into menopause knowing nothing—not even that I was in it. Like so many women who have always enjoyed good health and who prided themselves, upon reaching their mid-forties, on having achieved a fair degree of control over their lives, I was sure I would just "sail right through it." Instead, I veered off course, lost some of the wind in my sails, and almost capsized.

But in trying to learn or to talk about menopause, I found myself up against a powerful and mysterious taboo. My friends were adrift in the same fog. We couldn't help one another because none of us knew enough. Or we didn't want to know. It was as though we had been living with a conspiracy of silence. Ironically, that silence had served to hide how much power older women potentially wield.

In 1993 alone, it seemed that every time one picked up a newspaper another woman of menopausal age was assuming a position of command: U.S. Ambassador Madeleine

Albright (at fifty-six), shaping world policy at the United Nations; Janet Reno (at fifty-five), balancing the scales of justice as America's first female attorney general; Ruth Bader Ginsburg (at sixty), once the backseat wife encouraging her husband to go to law school, stepping up to the Supreme Court bench. And a whole new class of congresswomen, most of them in their fifties, won seats as freshwomen legislators in the nation's capitol. Clearly, contemporary women now moving into their fifties are transforming the whole concept of middle life.

As I traveled around the United States after the initial publication of *The Silent Passage*, giving lectures and appearing on TV and radio talk shows, the conversation about menopause had to be started up from scratch in each city. The effort was tantamount to breaking the ice at a particularly stiff cocktail party, the kind where everyone knows the host has just lost his job or his wife is having an affair, but nobody mentions it. Reactions from male talk show hosts were sometimes comical.

"Menopause," gulped a Cleveland man on the midday news. "Is that like—impotence?"

"Um, no," I murmured lamely. Only later did I think of the right comeback:

"Baldness. Is that like—Alzheimer's?"

When I appeared on the *Oprah* show, Oprah Winfrey's producer admitted that they had had an easier time booking guests to talk about murdering their spouses than about menopause. With tongue in cheek I suggested, "Why not have them both on the same show? They're probably the same people."

Six months after the conversation opened in the United States, menopause had become one of the hottest topics in the media, in bookstores, and on the lecture circuit. The silence, at last, was being broken. How that sea change came about, and what it promises for the improvement of women's health in general, is a wonderful example of what women can accomplish together.

The wellsprings of a new consciousness go back almost five years. In 1991, women of science who joined the U.S. government made a startling discovery. In the laboratories of the National Institutes of Health—clearinghouse for the testing of drugs that would supposedly benefit all Americans —there were no female rats in the cages. Only male rats. This was more than an odd preference for same-sex coworkers on the part of male researchers. It was the tip-off that women were not being represented in clinical trials. Medications designed to reduce heart disease, for example, were all tailored to male body chemistry. Yet heart disease was the major killer of women over fifty. And nobody had even looked into the impact of menopause on women's health.

All that began to change as the first tier of women from the formerly "Silent Generation" assumed high policy-making positions and changed the politics of menopause. Senator (then Congresswoman) Barbara Mikulski drove hard legislatively to make certain that brand-new offices dedicated to women's health were set up in the country's major public health agencies. Dr. Healy was no sooner named director of NIH than she spearheaded the Women's Health Initiative (WHI), the largest clinical study of women's health in American history. Taking advantage of the glare of publicity, Congresswoman Patricia Schroeder and the Congressional Women's Caucus pushed for the first subcommittee hearing on the role of menopause and disease in April 1991.

When I testified at that hearing, I was struck by the convergence of these brave point women and a bold new generation of baby boom women who were just approaching the brink of menopause. Better informed and less inhibited about their bodies all along, boomer women were not prepared to sit back and silently suffer like the women of Barbara Bush's generation. For my part, after some thought I decided to break the silence and go public with my own, not uncommon, experience and eventually found other well-known women willing to do the same. Initially, Tina Brown, then the editor of *Vanity Fair*, and Elise O'Shaughnessy, took the bold step of publishing my material. The electrifying response to that article was the impetus to expand my research and interviews into a book.

By the Nineties, American women wielded enough influence as scientists, physicians, nurses, legislators, journalists, and magazine editors that when they threw their weight behind opening up this subject in Congress and in the media, a huge wave of interest in menopause spread throughout society. We all seem to have discovered at the same time that we had an appalling lack of basic knowledge about this universal female transition. More pointedly, we had almost no hard data on the safety and efficacy of the hormone therapy routinely prescribed to millions of women—perhaps the largest uncontrolled clinical trial in the history of medicine. The lack of data at our National Institutes of Health was brought to public attention by government employees like Dr. Susan Blumenthal. A new position was created for her by President Clinton, who named her assistant surgeon general for women's health.

"It's shocking that it's taken until 1994 to launch the first major study of estrogen replacement therapy, through the Women's Health Initiative," says Secretary Blumenthal.

But we are catching up fast. Over one thousand women's health clinics have sprouted across the U.S. The demographics are impossible to ignore:

By now, forty-six million American women are in or beyond the age of menopause today (over age forty-five). And their numbers are projected to surge to nearly fifty million by the year 2000. More than one-third of all women in the U.S. have already passed their fiftieth birthday. Their sheer number may at last confer normalcy on this predictable passage.

This changes the politics of menopause drastically. Women's health activists have acquired such a large constituency among this not-so-silent majority of midlife women that drug companies and federal regulatory agencies now must listen to them. We are all learning as we go. As a member of the advisory board to the Women's Health Initiative, it is my privilege to serve with some of the most prominent physicians and scientific researchers in the field of menopause today and to learn from them. Even though the earliest results from WHI will not be available until the year 2000, the pooling of professional experience and probing questions generated by this group are already helping to raise the level of awareness within our scientific establishment.

In the meantime there are promising results from a three-year government-supported study of 875 women, known as the PEPI trial (Postmenopausal Estrogen/Progestin Intervention), which has already changed significantly the way hormone replacement therapy is prescribed. (Results of this study are discussed in the chapter "The PEPI Study Breakthrough.")

But there is an impetus even more basic than demographics or politics behind the massive shift in attitudes surrounding menopause. It is a revolution in the life cycle. As I describe in my latest book, *New Passages: Mapping Your Life Across Time*, in the space of one short generation the whole shape of the life cycle has been fundamentally altered. Middle age has already been pushed far into the fifties—if it is acknowledged at all today. The territory of the fifties, sixties, and beyond is changing so radically that it now opens up whole new passages leading to stages of life that are nothing like what our parents or grandparents experienced.

Fifty is what forty used to be.

When Barbara Bush says, from her perspective as a grandmother now in her seventies, "I was just the right age, fifty-one years old, for menopause," it rings slightly quaint. We know from studies that women are entering the long menopause passage earlier today, as much as five years earlier. What's more, we can now break down the menopausal transition into several distinctly different phases.

The first phase—perimenopause—is the least understood and potentially most confusing and symptomatic. Perimenopause is the months or years of transition from the childbearing years to the complete cessation of menstrual cycles that is menopause. Women pass through perimenopause sometime between forty and fifty. The latest surveys reveal a surprising number of women in their early forties are perimenopausal—and often don't know it. Yet the perimenopause phase is when hormonal fluctuations are the most volatile and when women experience the greatest number of symptoms, compared with any other stage. So far, there has not been much research on perimenopause. Only recently have physicians begun to recognize perimenopause as a distinct stage before actual menopause, says Howard Zacur, M.D., Ph.D., director of the Johns Hopkins Estrogen Consultation Service. This recognition is essential in order for physicians to provide correct medical treatment.

Today the women in perimenopause are most likely to be holding down responsible jobs and to have young children still at home. Those in demanding careers usually accelerate their efforts between age forty-five and fifty, when one either "makes it" into the top ranks or levels off. Now this acceleration in the workplace is likely to coincide with the body's "pause" for menopause. As working women begin to experience embarrassing symptoms such as hot flashes and erratic bleeding, they will demand that more attention be paid to perimenopause. It will become a public health issue.

And doctors and researchers and drug companies, as well as women themselves, will have to deal with it.

But we are no longer alone in the silent passage. We don't have to suffer the shame and depression that overtook Barbara Bush. Today there is a whole new way to think about the change of life.

You can plan for your menopause the way pregnancies can be planned.

Let that idea sink in as you read this book. You can start planning by talking candidly with mentors who are older than you and by searching out information in books and magazines and from the women's health conferences that are now routinely held in most communities. You can also begin to establish a lifelong relationship with a doctor who has a genuine interest in mature women and who understands the necessity of treating them as partners.

Another new concept that permeates this revised edition is the idea of *customizing* your approach to menopause. Menopause is like a thumbprint. No two women experience it alike. Some wonder what all the fuss is about, since they scarcely register any physical change. Others are bombarded by so many inexplicable symptoms, they wonder if they're going crazy. And many are misdiagnosed—sent off to see a neurologist or a cardiologist or a psychiatrist. Such blind alleys can be avoided with a little effort.

Each one of us has to examine our own thumbprint— that is, collect the information about our family's health history and consciously prepare ourselves for menopause. (See the section "The Menopause Gateway.") Each woman will have to decide for herself whether or not the benefits of hormone therapy are worth the risks in her case. (See the chapter "Should I or Shouldn't I?") But once she has her own health profile clearly in mind, if she does decide to use hormones, a specific hormonal replacement regimen can be designed to meet her health needs. There are a number of different products and combinations that now have the full approval of our health agencies. Doctors can adjust doses and regimens for each woman to suit the reactions of her body. But we can't expect doctors to take all the responsibility for customizing treatment. We have to educate ourselves to be informed partners.

The important point is that women in the Change today have choices; they need not follow anybody's manifesto or accept a one-size-fits-all prescription. This book is meant to empower women by informing them of the many different ways they can protect their bodies and promote their mental well-being through menopause and beyond, so they can look forward to finding passions and purposes apart from being vessels of reproduction.

You can become master of your menopause.

Some of the stories herein are cautionary tales of embittered or self-deluding women. And some are snapshots of women who have given themselves every chance to live out the length of their days in full, rich ways. I hope the stories of the women in this book will act as a catalyst for honest conversations about the menopausal experience between mothers and daughters, wives and husbands, women and their doctors.

This book, then, has three purposes: First, to shatter the myths about menopause. Second, to emphasize that menopause is a health issue, and to coach women on how to educate themselves, their doctors, and the men in their lives. And finally, most important, I want to leave readers with another way to think about this stage of a woman's life—what I call the Second Adulthood.

I am happy to report that in the short time since the original publication of this book, a new camaraderie has developed among women who are full of juice, humor, and determination to turn this passage into a celebration. They are forming "fan clubs" to share experiences, swap tips, and develop directories of doctors who are knowledgeable (or at least educable) about menopause. In many ways, there has never been a better time in history to pass through menopause.

In that spirit California women asked me to pass along this motto, which is being hung up on more and more office walls:

> WOMEN DON'T HAVE HOT FLASHES
> THEY HAVE POWER SURGES!

—G.S.

Author's Note

~

A further word on method. In my research, I sought out women from all social levels and races and regions. I conducted intimate group interviews, as well as collected individual life histories, in places as dissimilar as Eugene, Oregon; Rochester, New York; Louisville, Kentucky; downtown Los Angeles and Beverly Hills in California; Queens and Manhattan in New York. Participants included privileged women and low-income government workers, women of color and white suburbanites, early-forties women anticipating the Change and women in their sixties who could look back on it with some perspective. I interviewed over one hundred women in various stages of menopause and have since talked with thousands more as lectures have taken me around the country.

More detailed medical information was also necessary to raise awareness among women as health consumers. I freely crossed disciplines, reaching beyond the obvious medical practitioners—gynecologists, breast surgeons, and internists—to endocrinologists, who study the hard science of hormones, and epidemiologists, who measure in large populations all the factors contributing to a condition like menopause. Additional light was shed on this complex life transition by interviews with research physiologists, neuro-scientists, psychologists, psychiatrists, and gerontologists; and practical approaches to coping with it were suggested by nutritionists and Chinese medicine doctors. For a larger historical and evolutionary perspective I consulted scholars in sociology and anthropology, historians, and primate researchers. I interviewed a total of ninety experts.

But I have not been altogether alone in my explorations. Dr. Patricia Allen, a gifted obstetrician-gynecologist in private practice in Manhattan and on the staff at New York Hospital–Cornell Medical Center, took an interest in my efforts—both as my personal doctor and as a professional committed to expanding health education for women. She introduced me to top specialists in related fields and took to the trenches with me to listen in on some of the group interviews in other parts of the country. It is an ongoing journey of discovery for both Dr. Allen and myself, as we constantly compare notes, reevaluate conventional wisdom, and probe new scientific findings for revised editions of *The Silent Passage*.

My thanks go to Dr. William J. Ledger, professor and chairman of the Department of Obstetrics and Gynecology at New York Hospital–Cornell Medical Center, to Dr. Jamie Grifo, a new-generation gynecologist and research scientist also at New York Hospital, and to Dr. Robert Lindsay, a leading research endocrinologist in the field of menopause medicine and a practitioner at Helen Hayes Bone Center, all of whom read the manuscript and added valuable sugges-tions and refinements. Trudy Bush, Ph.D., a University of Maryland and Johns Hopkins epidemiologist and one of the principal investigators in the PEPI study of hormone re-placement therapy, kept me well-informed of the implica-tions of this important research.

In Britain, Dr. Malcolm Whitehead, director of the Menopause Clinic of Kings College Hospital, London, and president of the International Menopause Society, together with his senior research fellow, Dr. Mike Ellerington, were mines of information on the state of research and treatment in the U.K. Dr. John Moran, a private gynecologist at the Hormonal Healthcare Centre on Harley Street, in London, was very helpful in sharing his experience of treating thousands of women over the course of fifteen years in menopause clinics. Dr. Denning Cai, a gifted Chinese medicine doctor in Tarzana, California, and Dr. Shyam S. Singha, a world-renowned homeopathic practitioner and teacher in England, added a nontraditional treatment perspective.

It has been my privilege to work with one of this country's most distinguished editors, Robert Loomis, and for this new, revised edition my editor at Pocket Books, Julie Rubenstein, has been a stimulating and supportive partner. It has also been my good fortune to have the tireless research assistance of Leora Tanenbaum.

The women who gallantly contributed their personal stories to this book are also my partners. Some of their names and backgrounds had to be altered, but others offered their real names. To each one I offer thanks for striking one more small blow for normalization of a proud stage of life.

The
Need to Know
and the Fear
of Knowing

$\mathcal{A}$ group of recognizably high-powered media women on the shady side of forty were spaced around the table between their husbands and lovers at a Washington dinner party when a single sentence shattered their well-groomed calm. It came out of the mouth of a stunning network newswoman who ordinarily speaks in ninety-second bursts of inside-the-Beltway shorthand.

"Okay, there are only two subjects worth talking about—menopause and face-lifts." It was as though a nine-hundred-pound gorilla had just jumped up on the table.

We think of ourselves as so liberated today that we can talk about anything. People will tell strangers about their abortions or alcoholism, even declare on national television that they are HIV positive with the AIDS virus, yet just let a man suggest to his sleepless, perspiry, weepy wife that her uncharacteristic moods and symptoms might have something to do with menopause; he's bound to get a blanket denial: "What are you talking about! I'm too young!"

Menopause may be the last taboo. The first friend to whom I mentioned the subject is a sultry-looking woman, then just fifty (pre-baby boom). She has always prided herself on her appearance and gained much of her status from creatively supporting her husband, a successful author who looks somewhat younger than she. I asked if she had ever talked with anyone about menopause.

"No. And I don't want to."

"Women don't bring up the subject around you?"

"One friend did," she said sourly. "I haven't seen her since."

Another friend, a public television producer whose natural temperament is appallingly calm, recalled with rueful laughter her first sign of the Change of Life. She was seated between two titans of industry at a high-protocol Park Avenue dinner party, the kind where the place cards look like tracings from the *Book of Kells*, and she was feeling particularly confident and pretty in her new black designer suit with its flattering white satin collar, when out of the blue a droplet of something hit her collar. Then another drop. What the—was the help dribbling wine? Could there be a leaky ceiling under all that gorgeous boiserie? Suddenly she noticed her husband's gaze turn to alarm from across the table: What horrible thing was happening to her? She put a hand to her face. Her forehead was wet as a swamp.

Oh, no, said her eyes, *not me!* as the moisture began running in rivulets down her face and slipping off her chin—*plop*—onto her pearly satin collar. *Should I pick up the white linen napkin and wipe my forehead?* She reached for the five-hundred-threads-per-inch napery, hesitated— *no, all the makeup will come off on the damn napkin*—when a few more plops fell into her décolletage. Frantic, she began dabbing at her face. Trying to pretend it wasn't happening, she turned to her dinner partner and began smiling and mopping, chatting and fanning, laughing at his jokes and dabbing, trying to keep up her end of the conversation while she wanted nothing more in this world than to disappear into the kitchen and tear off her clothes and open the freezer door—never mind that it was February—and just *stand there.*

She and her husband have since had the Thermostat Wars usual in menopausal households—"It's freezing in here!" "No, it's boiling." "Did you turn the thermostat below fifty again?" "Oh, why don't you just get flannel pajamas!" But the producer is one of the lucky ones: She has had no other indicators beyond hot flashes that she is passing into another stage of life.

It happens to every woman. Pregnancy we can choose to go through or not. With menopause there is no choice. It happens to teachers and discount-store clerks and dental hygienists, who nonetheless have to function in public, on their feet, every day. It happens to Navy pilots and gray-haired graduate students and former Olympic athletes, who are accustomed to demanding the highest physical and mental performance from themselves. It happens to women of color and to women in the home. It happens even in Hollywood. Raquel and Ann-Margret and Candice Bergen, too, must deal with menopause. These women are hardly over the hill. In fact, they are hitting a new stride.

But they never mention the big M.

The central myth is that menopause is a time in a woman's life when she goes batty for a few years—subject to wild rages and deep depressions—and after it she mourns her lost youth and fades into the woodwork. In truth, menopause is a bridge to the most vital and liberated period in a woman's life. Certainly hormones have a powerful effect on our physical life and our mood, just as hormones underlie male aggression and affect potency as men age. During the passage through menopause, when hormones are spiking and falling a few times every day, or possibly within an hour, many women do experience waves of fatigue and bouts of the blues. But that is very different from clinical depression. And, most important, it is temporary.

In fact, women in their fifties, once through menopause, have the lowest rates of clinical depression compared to women at any other stage of life. Depression actually subsides with age for women.

Ironically, the people who are the most evasive and unsympathetic about menopause tend to be women in their forties. Slouching toward the bridge to that unknown and frightening new territory of "postmenopausal woman," they may be "menophobic." Their own resistance to identifying with the stage of life beyond reproductivity is sometimes expressed in an uncharacteristic intolerance of their own friends.

A thirty-nine-year-old Chicago woman moved to a new city the year her premature menopause came on. Although she made new friends quickly, they began to shun her as soon as she mentioned physical signs associated with the Change of Life. The ostracized woman struggled through five years with a large fibroid cyst, digestive problems, eating only mashed potatoes, and losing twenty pounds, before her friends and doctors acknowledged the source of her difficulties.

"I clearly remember not being sympathetic," recalled one of her friends with considerable regret. Others of the woman's friends admitted their impatience. "We'd talk about her among ourselves: 'She's complaining about hot flashes and stomach problems again this week. Why doesn't she just get over it?' We never really said, 'She's suffering.' We certainly never mentioned the possibility of menopause. And here we are, *women*."

"Women can be the worst," acknowledged her best friend.

The formerly shunned woman now realizes, "People

wouldn't relate my problems to menopause because that would automatically classify them as old."

Menopause must be one of the most misunderstood passages in a woman's life. One study showed that two thirds of all American women say nothing to anybody as they approach what may be a distressing and even fearsome Change. But who can blame us? Menopause is inextricably linked with middle age. In the youth-oriented societies of North America and Europe, even the mention of middle age has a stigma about it. Shame, fear, and misinformation are the vague demons that have kept us silent about a passage that could not be more universal among females. The most common fears are: *I'll lose my looks, I'll lose my sex appeal, I'll get depressed, I'll become invisible.* We don't have to lose any of these things. Yet the obvious sources of information and comfort—mothers, doctors, the media, academics—have shied away from the subject. All that is beginning to change. The subject of menopause is becoming part of our public conversation.

In a recent Gallup Poll, 44 percent of the women surveyed said they were satisfied with the information they received on menopause from their physicians. But for every woman who rates her health professional as very helpful, there is another woman who says he or she was not helpful at all, according to a more detailed and larger survey by *Prevention* magazine. "These women are saying they want to know more, to have a dialogue with their doctors," says Fredi Kronenberg, Ph.D., director of menopause research at the Center for Women's Health at Columbia-Presbyterian Medical Center in New York City.

Menopause is no longer a marker that means This Way to The End. Today fifty is the apex of the female life cycle. And today, menopause is more properly seen as the gateway to a *second adulthood*, a series of stages never before part of the predictable life cycle for other than the very long-lived.

If forty-five is the old age of youth, fifty is the youth of a woman's second adulthood. In fact, we can anticipate at least as many years of life after menopause as we have already lived as reproductive women. You don't believe it, do you? Consider. Most women begin menstruating around thirteen and begin stopping at around forty-eight—remaining defined, and confined, to some degree, by their procreative abilities for thirty-five years. The life expectancy of a woman fortunate enough to live to age fifty in the U.S. or U.K. is now eighty-one. (A man of fifty can expect to live until seventy-six.) So, from the time she reaches perimenopause, the average woman has thirty-three more years.

And an increasing number of women are living into advanced old age. A healthy, fifty-year-old American woman who does not succumb to heart disease or cancer can expect to see her *ninety-second birthday*, according to Kenneth Manton, Ph.D., a research professor of demographic studies at Duke University. Since there has been virtually no period in the history of the human species when evolution has favored postmenopausal females, we shall have to favor ourselves. We shall *have to* intervene—medically, hormonally, psychologically, spiritually—because we cannot assume that aging will go smoothly. Evolution didn't provide for it.

The main point is that we are living longer lives than ever before. But my impression from talking to thousands of women all over America and Europe is that this new perspective—only milliseconds old in evolutionary terms—has not caught up with most people.

Women today often believe they are well-informed about menopause. But the majority of women regard menopause as a short-term event and do not connect it with long-term health problems in postmenopausal life, such as heart disease, osteoporosis, or cancer. Fewer than half the women in a recent Gallup survey related the Change to these important issues, and more than one in four did not see a doctor at all, because they felt their symptoms were a natural part of menopause.

A keen social observer, British novelist Fay Weldon, points to the psychology of these women: "They'd on the whole rather not know—for if we don't know, it doesn't matter." But it does matter. It matters whether or not a woman in her sixties finds it painful to walk or even bend as a result of osteoporosis. It matters when a woman in her fifties has a heart attack. It matters that women look these possibilities in the eye, because the way in which they approach menopause will affect the risk of their suffering from these diseases. Naturally, parts of our bodies are going to break down with the aging process. Since many of us can expect to live into our eighties or nineties—whether we wish to or not—do we want to have bones and hearts that break down while the rest of us keeps going?

Menopause must be approached today with a different attitude, one that is self-valuing, rather than self-deprecating. Making the effort to change eating, smoking, sleeping, and exercise habits, or taking the time to experiment with hormone replacement or homeopathic practices to help rebalance the body around its new hormonal state, is not an issue of vanity, or attracting men, or succumbing to Western culture's preoccupation with youth. It is an issue of physical and mental *health*.

It is time to render normalcy to a normal physical process that ushers in the youth of our Second Adulthood. This is a passage as momentous as the rite of passage into adolescence. Indeed, the menopausal passage is almost the mirror image of the transition to adolescence for females, and it will take just as many years. Jolted into menstruating at twelve or thirteen—remember?—it took five years or more for our bodies to adjust to our uniquely altered chemistry, while our minds struggled to incorporate our new self-image. So, too, must we readjust to *not* menstruating.

The Silent Passage: menopause

Just as we were apprehensive as eleven-year-olds, standing on the doorsill of childhood, about to be pushed out into the unknown turbulence of puberty, so are we naturally nervous at the approach of menopause, about letting go of aspects of femininity that have defined us. We become more acutely aware of health, appearance, economic security, and the harbingers of mortality.

I know what you're thinking. *Thank God this is a book that I don't have to read.* Because you're not fifty yet, or even close. That's the first misconception.

"You're Not Old Enough"

Linda Lavin, in her role as Edie Kurland on ABC's series *Room for Two*, opened the window to this subject on prime time TV in 1993 when she did an episode entitled "A Pause for Menopause." From *Roseanne* to *Murphy Brown*, sitcoms are beginning to reverberate with menopause humor. Women are writing novels and producing films that encompass the rite of passage that transforms them from childbearers to wisewomen. As healthy as it is to laugh about our situation, sitcoms come and go once a week. Menopause has a habit of hanging around.

Menopause is arbitrarily defined as "the final cessation of menstruation," as if it were a single point in time when the switch is turned off on those fabulous egg-ripening machines, the ovaries. In fact, it's a much more gradual, stop-start series of pauses in ovarian function that are part of that mysterious process called aging. (A more comprehensive term is the *climacteric*, for which there is a male counterpart.) We are born with all the eggs we'll ever have, about seven hundred thousand. Each month after puberty, one ovary offers up a selection of from twenty to one thousand mature eggs, though usually only one is released into the fallopian tube to meet any sperm in the vicinity. As we get close to the bottom of the egg basket, ovulation doesn't always take place. The quality of egg follicles that month may be substandard, or there may not be sufficient estrogen manufactured by the ovaries. When the supply of viable eggs is gone, menstruation stops completely and the fertile period of a woman's life ends.

The median age at which women in Western countries stop ovulating altogether is 50.8. But today there are no clear age cues as to when the long transition begins or when it ends. "For a long time we've thought of menopause as a very sudden event—it really isn't," says Dr. Trudy Bush, epidemiologist at the University of Maryland and at Johns Hopkins School of Hygiene and Public Health. "The ovaries start producing less estrogen probably in the mid-thirties. There's a gradual loss of estrogen production and other hormones until the ovaries finally stop putting out very much estrogen at all. It's not uncommon to see symptoms in the early forties as a sign of gradual estrogen withdrawal."

Eight women out of every one hundred undergo a natural menopause *before age forty*, according to renowned reproductive endocrinologist Dr. Lila Nachtigall, director of the Women's Wellness Division at New York University Medical School. The youngest case on record was seen at Kings College Hospital: a nineteen-year-old girl.

Increasingly, say veteran practitioners, the American women turning up in menopause clinics are younger by four or five years than in the recent past. Researchers now admit they have underestimated the number of younger women who experience all the symptoms of menopause even though they still have periods. Some speculate that in the past, when women had many pregnancies, they had an easier menopause. As middle-class Western women we have changed our lifestyle—postponing childbirth, having fewer children, synthetically controlling our menstrual cycle, and often introducing fertility drugs, or having tubes tied or a uterus surgically removed—and we may be throwing our hormonal systems out of balance.

My own younger sister started missing periods when she was forty-three—five years earlier than it began with me. One month her "little friend" would come, then not again for another two or three months, whereupon it would reappear, only to disappear again. After half a year of this, feeling poorly, she called her gynecologist and popped the obvious question: "Is this the beginning of menopause?"

"No," he stated categorically. "You're not old enough."

It's tempting to take this bromide so commonly dispensed by physicians and to go away feeling smug and secure in one's continuing fecundity. Isn't it reassuring to know that you're still young? Well, not young exactly, but still, in some respect at least, *underage*.

"I started very early, at forty," I was told by another woman I'll call Barbara, a delightfully wise Oregonian with a thriving psychotherapy practice. "It was no fun. I was blown away by the hot flashes. I felt enormous restlessness and cranky, cranky, cranky!" Her doctor, too, said she wasn't old enough to take estrogen. Or, as she heard it, she hadn't suffered enough.

A roaring extrovert, Barbara stood up to her full five feet nine inches and stared down her doctor. "Either you give me estrogen, or the next time I have a hot flash I'm going to rip my clothes off and shout your name!"

The man dispensed the pills and preserved his anonymity. But once on hormones, Barbara blew up. "I gained five pounds a year for six years until I finally said the hell with it. I quit taking the estrogen, and I have all the lines in my face to show for it." Now in her early fifties, she does look parched and abruptly elderly. "You age faster after menopause," she concludes, though it would be more accurate to say that one ages faster after any *abrupt* withdrawal from hormones.

On the opposite end, women may never be quite sure when, or if, they have finished with menopause. This is particularly true for women who go right onto hormone therapy at the first signs of the Change and continue having periods as if they were still reproductive. There is no noticeable evidence of when they stop ovulating, no clear metaphysical marker that they are moving beyond fertility into another stage of life.

Margaret Mead originated the memorable phrase *post-menopausal zest.* Yet Mary Catherine Bateson, the daughter of the pioneering anthropologist, is still puzzled about when her own mother actually became menopausal. When Dr. Mead reached the age of forty-eight and probably experienced the first hot flashes, she persuaded her doctor to try giving her shots of estrogen, the primary female hormone, telling him it was for a circulatory problem. "And it worked," she noted in a brief medical history made available to me by her daughter, an anthropological researcher and author in her own right. At age fifty-three Dr. Mead noted "longer space between periods and lighter flow." But she continued to have hormone-induced periods for another eight years, whereupon she asserted that she had held off menopause until her sixties.

To add to the age blurring, vanguard baby boomers are giving birth to yet another phenomenon unique to their generation: *menopause moms.* A woman I'll call Sondra had been involved in SDS at Columbia—"a classic Sixties person," as she described herself. She spent the next fifteen years as a politically obsessed radical in "movement work," followed by a very respectable marriage and a cascade of miscarriages. Sondra was forty-two by the time she finally produced her first baby. That was two years ago.

"Thank God I finished breast-feeding just in time for

menopause," she deadpanned. She swears she felt hot flashes while she was breast feeding (a normal occurrence).

Already, the boardrooms of America are lighting up with hot flashes. The point women among the baby boomers, those now in their mid-forties who are the first among their generation to approach the passage into menopause, are probably operating at 110 percent. They may be in command positions in their professional lives, or starting over to get a graduate degree, while also feeling a new sense of social obligation. Those who have remained childless and have conflicted feelings about it can turn their caregiving instincts outward. The married ones have a new chance for romance with a neglected husband if the nest is now empty; the divorced or widowed ones may choose to savor their independence or delight in a new love or a new sexual orientation. But at the same time, many women over forty-five are likely to be sandwiched between an abruptly dependent parent or in-law who is entering the twilight of ill health and the continued dependence of children who today remain adolescent until the end of their twenties— and even move back in! This is no time suddenly to find one can't sleep, or can't shake the blues, or can't call up facts memorized the day before.

Most educated women today expect to take control of this annoying little disruption. After all, they have been accustomed to birth control and using technology to correct and control problems with fertility. No wonder so many are thrown into a fit when their bodies unexpectedly backfire on them.

Psychologist Ellen McGrath, a vivacious and experienced media spokeswoman in her mid-forties and a good friend of mine, was preparing to go out on her first book tour. She was petrified. For three years she had drawn on all her physical and mental resources to produce her magnum opus on depression, a book for the popular market titled *When*

Feeling Bad Is Good. Now she had to go out and sell it; no tryouts out of town, she had to open on a national breakfast TV show before an audience of five million.

"The week before the tour, suddenly I couldn't remember my material. Pieces of it would just go. I thought, 'My God, my mind is the main thing I have. What's happening to me?'" Ellen had recently been having trouble sleeping, feeling vaguely hot but without sweating. Earlier, I had shared with her some of my research. "Though I never thought it would apply to me, I had some hunch of what this could be, and a name for my malaise—menopause." So she asked her doctor to fit her in immediately and had a blood test done to measure her hormone levels. "Turns out, I wasn't just in perimenopause. I had gone straight into full menopause, at forty-six!" The doctor gave her an injection of a megadose of estrogen to hold her over for several months. "The astounding thing was, my symptoms disappeared within forty-eight hours," says Ellen.

But after this quick fix, those symptoms reappeared with a vengeance. Ellen was enraged. "I don't have time to deal with this!" she insisted. Having recently been there myself, I knew exactly how she felt: she was losing some of the control she'd fought so hard to gain. It's particularly dispiriting to feel a loss of control over something so elemental as our bodies.

"But you can't run away from it," I tried to tell Ellen. "What you have to do at this stage is go home. Listen to your body. Take the pause—you've earned it."

My friend couldn't buy my argument. Not then, at any rate. She had a right to her anger and denial. These are normal, predictable reactions to the first phase of menopause, especially for the achieving women of the baby boom. You will be angry, embarrassed, impatient, and incredulous that this could happen to you. You may believe that if you do "give in" to menopause, your identity will

16

disintegrate, along with your body, and you will turn into a dried-up old crone overnight.

You are not alone. Hundreds of women I have interviewed felt the same way at the outset of this passage. The late forties often represent the pits for women, while the early fifties usually find them at their peak. Before one breaks into that most productive stage of life, one must accept losses of certain cherished strengths that were fundamental to our identity in young adulthood. Everyone feels anger and frustration at physical changes in the body. For women, these losses are further accentuated by menopause, which also entails letting go of the godlike powers of reproduction.

"When I turned fifty, I cried a lot," said a New York businesswoman. "You have to grieve, and then when you come out on the other side, it feels very liberating."

Singer-songwriter Joni Mitchell described to me the pits-to-peak course of her passage in much the same way. "I went over the hump of the middle-life crazies. There is a kind of mourning period for those things you can no longer do. But then something happened of its own accord. You can feel a chemical change in your body, as you go over that hump. You have a greater ability to let go and say, 'I don't want to think about that now,' which is the thing I always admired about men."

There is another reason that menopause is no longer clearly age-linked today. More than one-third of the women in the United States have hysterectomies —thirty-seven women out of one hundred—an astounding figure. (North America leads the world in numbers of hysterectomies, with twice as many as in Great Britain.) The majority of these women have hysterectomies between the ages of twenty-five and forty-four. A classical hysterectomy, which means removal of the uterus and cervix, even *without removal of the ovaries*, usually brings on an early menopause, within two years of the surgery. Removal of the ovaries, called oophorectomy, brings on menopause immediately, no matter how young a woman is.

This is all part of a fundamental change in the way we view the adult life cycle of women. *The biological transition of menopause is no longer an age-tied marker event.*

But no matter when the first awareness dawns on a woman that menopause might be imminent for her, it comes as a shock. Virtually nothing prepares most women for this mysterious and momentous transition. Indeed, some of us unconsciously tell ourselves, "It's not going to happen to me."

When You Least Expect It

〜

$\mathcal{N}$o more incongruous time or place could be imagined, the night I was hit by the first bombshell of the battle with menopause. It was a Sunday evening. Snug inside a remarriage not yet a year old, I was sitting utterly still, reading, in a velvet-covered armchair. A pillow's throw away my husband was doing the same, while jazz lapped at our ears and snow curtained the window. Every so often we looked up and congratulated ourselves on staying home in this cocoon of comfort and safeness and love we had created.

Then the little grenade went off in my brain. A flash, a shock, a sudden surge of electrical current that whizzed through my head and left me feeling shaken, nervous, off-balance.

"What was that?" I must have mumbled.

"What?"

"Nothing."

But some powerful switch had been thrown. I tried to go back to reading. It was difficult to concentrate. When I looked down at the pages I had just finished, I realized the imprint of their content on my brain had washed out. I felt hot, then clammy. I tried lying down, but sleep could not soak up the agitation. My heart was racing, but from what? Complete repose? I felt, for perhaps the first time in my life since the age of thirteen, profoundly ill at ease inside my body.

In the months that followed, I sometimes felt *outside* my body. I was aware of spates of "static" in my brain and came to recognize the aura that preceded the first migraine-like headaches I'd ever had. Usually optimistic, I began having little bouts of blues. Then little crashes of fatigue. Having always counted on abundant energy, it was profoundly upsetting to find myself sometimes crawling home from a day of writing and falling into bed for a "nap," from which I had to drag myself up just to have dinner.

I was only forty-eight. And still menstruating. So this couldn't be "Change of Life," could it?

Besides, all these strange physical sensations were only background noise in what was otherwise a thrilling, adrenaline-pumping, mind-stretching period of creative redirection, in both my career and my new family life. I was traveling all over the country and the world and coming home to a husband and new adopted child, both of whom I adored, satisfied that another beloved daughter was already launched. So I took Scarlett's "fiddle-dee-dee" approach; I'd think about it tomorrow.

But "tomorrow" I began to notice something strange. For the first time since my early teens, when the sexual pilot light went on and I was warned not to want sex too much, I began to worry about not wanting it enough. Again, I had the sensation of standing outside my body and scolding it: "What's the matter with you—why don't you *act* the way I feel anymore?"

I went to see my conservative, male gynecologist, known as a superb clinician but short on communication skills. He measured my hormone levels. I was very low on estrogen. I vaguely remembered my family doctor having mentioned in passing, when he'd rattled off the results of my annual physical in recent years, that my estrogen levels were getting lower and lower.

"Could I be a candidate for hormone replacement therapy?" I asked.

"Not yet." My gynecologist went strictly by the book. "You're not in menopause, because you're still menstruating. You have to be menstruation-free for a year before I can give you estrogen replacement."

"But this, um, effect on my sexual response"—embarrassed, I fumbled for the words—"couldn't that be because I need more estrogen, like a vitamin supplement?"

"It's nothing I can help you with. Decrease in sexual response is just a natural part of aging."

The curt clinician washed his hands of me. I left his office feeling as though I'd just been handed a one-way ticket to the Dumpster. *Does this mean I can't be me anymore?*

It was time for me to shop for another gynecologist. A recommendation sent me to see Patricia Allen, a vivacious woman in her forties and an attending physician at New York Hospital who demands excellence of herself and discipline from her patients. She made it clear from the start that she does not accept passive patients or women who smoke, only those who are willing to participate actively in their own health care. That sounded reasonable. She spent a good twenty minutes before the physical exam taking a holistic history. The irregular periods, the erratic expanding and constricting of blood vessels that caused the static, and the mood swings indicated to her that I was in perimenopause. Then she said something startling:

"I believe in treating each patient as an individual. This perimenopausal period should be a transformation, so that a woman gets to become—physically, emotionally, and spiritually—the best that she ever was." Imagine your run-of-the-mill male gynecologist harboring such a radical point of view!

Dr. Allen posited that the impact of low estrogen on me, as on many women, was emotional. Of the several hundred patients who consult her about managing their menopause, quite a few mention feeling depressed although they have no rational reason to be. She also took seriously my distress over changes in libido. She asked if there was a history of osteoporosis in my family, which brought to mind memories of my mother suffering in her seventies as she sat on her powdery bones.

All in all, Dr. Allen felt I was a good candidate for hormone therapy, but she drove a strict bargain with her patients. Estrogen by itself carries a known increase in the risk of cancer of the endometrium—the lining of the uterus—which is sloughed during menstrual periods. So she also prescribed a progestin* (synthetic progesterone), to protect against that risk. Also, I would have to agree to have an endometrial biopsy several months later to detect any changes in the tissue. She urged me to have a bone density evaluation done ($250), as well as a mammogram. This complete diagnostic workup cost $800, much of which was reimbursable by health insurance. It was costly, but it turned out to be part of an investment in long-term health and productivity that has more than paid for itself— and one I would recommend for all women who can afford it.

I filled the standardized prescription for 0.625 mg of Premarin (estrogen made from pregnant mares' urine, from which it derives its unforgettable name) and 10 mg tablets of Provera, the progesterone that stimulates the sloughing of the uterine lining. This is an approximation of the two hormones that the body produces naturally in the reproductive years.

---

*The terms are so similar as to be endlessly confusing: Progesterone refers to the natural hormone made by the body to control the action of estrogen; a progestin is any one of the synthetic equivalents; and just to drive you crazy, Europeans call their synthetics progestogens.

After only a month, the estrogen had rekindled sexual desire, stopped the surges of static and dips of fatigue, and chased away the blues. But the Provera was another matter. It brought on physical and emotional symptoms that I'd never experienced before. After a year of the combined hormones, my body seemed to be at war with itself for half of every month. My energy was flagging, and resistance to minor infections was falling. I felt as if I were racing my motor. So I stopped taking hormones cold turkey.

Dr. Allen agreed it was a good idea to take a break and see how the body responded. If nothing else, she said, going off hormones often serves to remind women why they started taking them in the first place.

For the first two months off hormones I felt marvelous; the bloating disappeared, as did the induced periods, and the terrible cramps and tension and sleeplessness that had begun to accompany them. I even got my waist back. Then, a crash. All the perimenopausal phenomena returned with exaggerated force. Now the static became full-fledged hot flashes and night sweats that interrupted sleep and left me limp by morning. I went back to my estrogen pills.

Within days the "blue-meanie" moods lifted. I was able to write for twelve hours straight on deadline and remain calm and reasonable under crisis. Within a few weeks all the other complaints were gone. I was staggered by the potency of the female hormone.

But the impact of the progesterone was also intensified. On day fifteen, when I had to add the Provera pills to my regimen, I felt by afternoon as if I had a terrible hangover. This chemically induced state was not to be subdued by aspirin or a walk in the park. It only worsened as the day wore on, bringing with it a racing heart, irritability, waves of sadness, and difficulty concentrating. And to top it off, the hot flashes came back! Cramps introduced pain for a week at a time. By night I couldn't go to sleep without a glass of wine, and even then was awakened by a racing heartbeat and sweating. *Won't I ever be me anymore?*

It didn't require a ten-year clinical trial and double-blind study to guess what was going on. Taking synthetic progesterone with the estrogen for half of each month was like pushing down the gas pedal and putting on the brakes at the same time, and it had left my body confused and worn out.

Clinicians I later interviewed relayed common side effects reported by patients who were taking the drug: "Whenever I take Provera, I have migraines, bloating, breast tenderness, the blues. I feel awful and want to die." As more than one woman has said to me, "Why am I going through this for ten days a month? Who needs it?"

The good news is women today don't have to go through the lengthy and painful experimentation that I had to—if they are well-informed. For one thing, perimenopausal women are now much more likely to ask for and receive treatment for disruptive symptoms. In the *Prevention* survey, "We found it especially interesting that so many perimenopausal women (40 percent) had tried hormones," says Dr. Cristina Matera, assistant professor of clinical obstetrics and gynecology at Columbia University. "That's a change in the way physicians approach hormone-replacement therapy."

You can now custom-design your own hormone replacement therapy. The Food and Drug Administration (FDA) has recently approved at least two options of hormone replacement therapy (HRT). One is the old cyclical regimen that I've just described, which works fine for some people; the other is the newer, continuous regimen that proved itself in the PEPI trial. (For a full discussion of HRT alternatives see the chapters "The PEPI Study Breakthrough" and "Should I or Shouldn't I?")

Premarin is now the most widely used prescription drug by American women. Sales of estrogen products were up 11 percent in 1994 and are now nearing a billion dollars a year. The baby boom bulge shifted eight-hundred-thousand women into the target group in 1992 and is projected to add over a half million women to the midlife population each year for the rest of the decade. The menopause market is becoming big business.

To come up with a safe and intelligent custom design for your menopause, however, means you will have to do most of the work—or, at the very least, find a doctor who is making a special effort to keep abreast of developments in this rapidly changing area of medicine. Hormone replacement therapy is taken by 27.5 percent of American women age forty-five and over who are menopausal, a significant increase over the last several years. The numbers have also increased in Great Britain, where two years ago only 9 percent of women with menopausal symptoms were on hormone replacement therapy; today the number is 20 percent.

Many women, however, are woefully ignorant about the intelligent questions to ask a doctor. Even after you do some research or experimentation and find the solution for you, it is still important to keep up to date on the research findings coming out. The bottom line is, what is right for you today might have serious consequences five years from now; so make sure you are aware of them and that your doctor is aware of them. If a man has a heart attack, his doctor has all the pertinent research at his fingertips. This is not the case with hormone replacement therapy. Women have to better protect themselves against being hormonal guinea pigs.

Deal or Deny?

$\mathcal{M}$y experience is not abnormal. Almost all women experience some menopausal symptoms, but few have severe problems. An estimated 20 percent sail through with little difficulty and another 10 percent or so are temporarily incapacitated. The rest of us—70 percent of all women—wrestle to some degree with difficulties that come and go over a period of years as we deal with the long transition from our reproductive state. (Data going back to the nineteenth century are consistent: Almost all women experience some menopausal symptoms, but few have severe problems.)

The menopause experience varies with genes, age, class, temperament, marital status, whether or not a woman has had children—everything. Antonia Fraser, the author of internationally acclaimed historical biographies, is a prime example of one of those fortunate women who are scarcely aware of the Change. When we met for lunch at the English Garden in London, I couldn't quite believe she had just turned sixty. A tall, strongly built woman who has borne six children and enjoyed a sexually robust past, Lady Antonia remains intensely feminine. From the gossamer blond hair fluffed around her face and the flirtatious sweep of her opaline blue eyes, she seems to sit very comfortably, and naturally, within her own skin. And enviable skin it is; "lucky genes" keep it glistening like dewed fruit. Fine tracings on either side of her lips and eyes are the only certain evidence of passing time. It isn't as though she has been resting on her laurels. She worked feverishly to finish her latest romantic historical biography, *The Six Wives of Henry VIII*, so that it could be published on her sixtieth birthday.

Some among the previous generation of women in her famous family had "floods" during menopause. Lady Antonia had expected it would be the same for her. "I didn't think it was worrying, it would just be extremely inconvenient." As it transpired, her cycle stopped at the age of forty-nine. No signs. "Nothing, except a slight tendency to throw open the windows for fresh air."

Being the beaverish historian that she is, Lady Antonia had checked her recollection with her husband, the playwright Harold Pinter, the night before our interview. "Am I fantasizing?" she asked. "He might have said, 'You were bloody hell.'"

But Pinter said, "No, you're not fantasizing." She never considered taking hormones, feeling no need. But she keeps up regularly with her former roommates from Oxford, and as they talked through menopause she learned there is a very wide range of experience. "One of my closest friends had a very bad time with depression," she recounts, "and was saved by HRT. Her looks certainly improved on the hormones." She smiles, self-deprecatingly. "You know, you can't help looking and comparing." Even fortunates like the aristocratic Lady Antonia, however, do have the long-term health impact of the Change to consider.

"Menopause is not a disease," says the epidemiologist Trudy Bush. "It's a life transition, but it carries with it a different internal hormonal milieu which is, in fact, detrimental to our bodies. When we don't have estrogen, our bones get brittle, our rates of heart disease go up, our vagina becomes less moist, our skin becomes dry and thin. In fact, we can reverse those processes that are related to the hormones rather than to aging per se."

Estrogen is involved in something like three hundred bodily processes. So, when it dips below levels one's body has come to rely upon as normal for thirty years or more, the body is naturally thrown out of balance. The brain's brain, the hypothalamus, cannot coordinate with its usual precision functions such as body temperature, metabolic rate, sleep cycle, blood chemistry, and so on.

Subtle influences on brain chemistry, similar to the experience of jet lag, may be a harbinger of perimenopause, for instance. The editor of the London *Sunday Express*, Eve Pollard, admits that she sometimes has a little more difficulty concentrating or remembering things these days. "I know I have to make lists, but then I'm running a magazine and a newspaper and trying to manage children and step-children as they get older, when you can't lay down the law anymore." In her second marriage, juggling two children and three step-children, Pollard may be in for a pleasant surprise.

All but about 10 percent of women, which represents the extreme, will succeed quite effectively throughout menopause at balancing their usual nine lives. But they must take the trouble to inform themselves, since no one else will. "All of us are quite ignorant," Pollard admits.

The temptation, of course, is to deny the signs. Or to give up on dealing with the larger passage because we can't find quick and easy answers to resolve the physical challenge of menopause. In talking to women all over the United States and Britain, I did find some significant differences in attitudes and reactions to menopause, depending on how women are valued in a particular subculture. But there was one strong common denominator: Women in midlife are still afraid to know—and fiercely resist acknowledging—that menopause can affect *them*, but at the same time, in spite of themselves, they are desperately anxious to learn what it's all about.

For millions of women in Britain the Change of Life remains a taboo subject. They endure it in silence, unable to discuss their fears even with their husbands. Only one in ten women approaching menopause confides in her spouse, according to a *Sunday Express* survey. Nearly two in three say nothing to anybody, including their GP, as they approach what may be one of the more distressing transitions in their lives.

Privately, women will go to extraordinary lengths to pick up information, cornering a researcher at a party and interrogating him or her, stealing books from doctors' offices—I was particularly proud to learn that *The Silent Passage* made the list of Ten Most Shoplifted Books in America—but heaven forbid that anyone should bring up the subject at the dinner table! Psychologist Abraham Maslow gave a name to this syndrome of ambivalence: "the need to know and the fear of knowing."

In fact, there is no single, risk-free solution that suits everyone. Menopause is highly idiosyncratic. Remember how different we were, one from another, as we entered puberty—some of us embarrassed still to be wearing undershirts at thirteen, while our best friend was turning into a hunchback to hide the pods suddenly swelling under her sweater? Well, the Change of Life is even more individual. Peggy Sue may tell you that she hardly noticed a thing. Her periods tapered off, she had a few hot flashes, but she sailed right through—no problem. Peggy Sue may be one of the lucky 10 or 15 percent of women who find the Change of Life uneventful. She may also be plump, or obese, and since estrogen is produced in the fat cells, this is one case where fat is more advantageous than thin. Or, she may be lying.

Whatever Peggy Sue's experience of the Change, it doesn't make your signs and symptoms any less true. The older we grow, the more unlike we are, one from another. Besides the changes in our brains and sexual characteristics over the years, our endocrine systems are different, our metabolisms are different, our blood vessels and bones become more dissimilar, depending on our lifetime eating and exercise habits. So it is not surprising that there is not one menopause; there are hundreds of variations.

But instead of giving in to frustration over dealing with our uniqueness, we can recognize how lucky we are. In all of human history women's lives were under the coercion of their biology. Today we don't have to be forty-five years old and suddenly estrogen-deficient, miserable, and without recourse. We have choices. And they don't all involve taking drugs, by any means.

The first step we can take toward mastering this stage of life is to describe the beast, give a shape and characteristics to it, and look it in the face. The actual derivation of the word menopause is from the Greek *meno*, meaning "month," and *pausis*, which is literally translated "ending," though more accurately it connotes a pause in the life cycle. The Change of Life is one of the three great "blood mysteries" that demarcate a woman's inner life, the earlier ones being menarche and pregnancy.

Despite the trial-and-error state of medical care, a woman at fifty now has a second chance. To use it, she must make an alliance with her body and negotiate with her vanity. Today's healthy, active pacesetters will become the pioneers, mapping out a whole new territory for potent living and wisdom-sharing from one's fifties to one's eighties and even beyond.

The Need to Know and the Fear of Knowing

Yet the reluctance to discuss both the trials and the rewards of moving through the Change of Life has obscured the facts, often keeping younger women in a state of menopausal dread. One naturally asks, *If menopause is such a significant passage to a whole new stage of life, why is it so neglected?*

Mother Doesn't Always Know Best

~

$\mathscr{I}$ don't know how to be fifty," one West Coast woman told me. "I'm not going to fifty like my mother, and there haven't really been any models."

Very rarely had any of the women I interviewed learned much about menopause from their own mothers. If they reported any mother-daughter conversation on the subject at all, the mothers' answers tended to be brief and evasive: "There was nothing to it; my periods just stopped"; or "I don't remember much about menopause." "When I asked my mother about menopause," said Effie Graham, a black nurse who grew up in the South, "all she said was, 'You'll find out when you get it.' She never told me about my period either."

A Gallup survey found that the majority of women get their "facts" about menopause from magazines, books, TV or newspapers, and friends, in that order. They seldom turn to their mothers. And the last person most women consult is a doctor; barely one third of women surveyed reported receiving menopausal information from their physicians.

One woman told a researcher she learned about menopause from Edith on an episode of *All in the Family.*

There are good reasons that the same mothers and mothers-in-law who assume possession of the revealed wisdom on child rearing are peculiarly scanty of expertise on this subject. The mothers of today's menopause-aged women came through the Depression and were an exceptionally prudish lot. It was shameful to discuss any bodily functions in their day.

And what was there to discuss about menopause? Our mothers had no information. No biomedical research had been done into the most pressing health questions of women as they age. Most of our mothers had no idea of the major killer diseases or disorders that would deprive them of a decent quality of life in their sixties, seventies, or eighties. And they certainly didn't know that their risk of being attacked by heart disease, hip fractures, and breast cancer was decidedly affected by the way they handled their Change of Life.

It is safe to assume most of our mothers never even heard the word *osteoporosis*—a silent disease caused by deterioration of the bone tissue—much less associated it with menopause. Only in the last five years or so has osteoporosis been identified as a crippler of life's quality, afflicting almost twenty-five million women. It leeches the very lining of our bones, like a colony of termites inside our foundations. Beginning their invisible destruction as soon as our supply of estrogen is depleted, these "termites" accelerate their robbing of mineral from our bones during the time around menopause.

Many women in their forties today are at the hub of several generations. Unless they're incapacitated, they feel too stretched for time and money to consult doctors or take expensive tests in order to manage their own menopause. In fact, most middle-class and low-income women don't consult any professional about how to protect their health and well-being during the Change of Life. If they adopt their mothers' attitudes without examination, they often blindly follow a path that, unbeknownst to the older women, may have been responsible for untold deficits of mental and physical well-being.

"My mother had a surgical menopause in her early forties," mentioned Gloria, a nurse from an Italian-American family, "so I really don't know much about it." Gloria herself had run into some mean symptoms starting in her forty-eighth year, which she refused to connect to menopause. "I was having terrible flashes, insomnia, I was very depressed," she described. "But I associated it with changing jobs." Although Gloria had successfully practiced pediatric nursing all her life, she found herself suddenly upset by the demands of sickly children. "I was crying all the time."

Others in the group interview asked if she had seen a doctor. "No," admitted the nurse. "I was going to coax myself out of it, be calm, take deep breaths." She explained that her mother had ingrained in her an aversion to taking any medicine, especially hormones.

Gloria had no idea if her own mother had been given estrogen after having her ovaries removed. "That's very private," she said, reflecting a common silence in families. "Even her sisters don't know." Gloria had been a nurse for almost thirty years, yet she had never stopped to wonder what it must have been like for her own mother to suffer the sudden depletion of hormones after a full hysterectomy, an experience often described as a nightmare. She had simply adhered to the voice of her inner dictator—perhaps replicating her mother's stoical misery—and denied herself permission to have any problems with the Change. In the process she almost lost her job. "I totally lost confidence in myself as a nurse," Gloria confessed. "And I didn't know that I would be able to conquer it."

In addition to lacking informed guidance from their

mothers, many women who are in the menopause years right now are handicapped by their own inhibitions. Born in the late Thirties or early Forties, they went through high school in the uptight Fifties, before the sexual revolution, before liberation, when only "bad girls" became sexually active before marriage, and a lot of others lied about it. Part of the "Silent Generation," they have never been comfortable talking about sexual matters. Their silence on the subject of menopause may now be an anachronism.

Evolution and the
Victorian Hangover

~

A nother reason for the mystery surrounding menopause is that human females today are monkeying with evolution. Most higher primates do not live long enough in the wild even to have a menopause; the phenomenon has never been clearly established in apes or monkeys, according to Dr. Kim Wallen, a researcher at Emory University's Yerkes Primate Center. Most female animals just go right on breeding until they roll over and die.

The same was true of human females for many thousands of years. At the turn of the century a woman could expect to live to the age of forty-seven or -eight. She bore an average of eight children, which kept her busy giving birth or nursing right up to menopause.

Nature, then, never provided for women who would routinely live several decades beyond the age of fifty. Once females had made their genetic contribution, evolution was finished with them, and society followed suit. In view of this historically powerful linkage of menopause with decline and death, is it any wonder that today's women approach fifty under a shadow of archetypal fears of being transformed, all at once, into an Old Woman?

The secrecy, shame, and ignorance that still veil this natural transition have carried over from the Victorian Age with very little mitigation of the punishing stereotypes. "Menopause in the nineteenth century was described only in terms of what women lose at this stage of life," says Marilyn Yalom, senior scholar at the Stanford University Institute for Research on Women and Gender. The Victorians were obsessed with women as reproductive creatures. Once barren and widowed, as they were likely to be by fifty, they were cued to view menopause as "the gateway to old age, through which a woman passed at the peril of her life." Yalom's chapter in the documentary text *Victorian Women* quotes nineteenth-century obstetricians who taught that "the change of life unhinges the female nervous system and deprives women of their personal charm." These attitudes were tempered somewhat by the sassy and energetic social activists who emerged between 1890 and 1920, a period that celebrated "the renaissance of the middle-aged." As death in childbirth was reduced, middle-class women began to appreciate the possibilities of a full life cycle and to cluster their childbearing in the earlier years of marriage. In their mature years they took up social causes, marched in parades, and founded movements. The great feminist leaders such as Elizabeth Cady Stanton celebrated the liberation of being in their fifties and continued as activists well into their sixties. *Cosmopolitan* magazine sang the praises of vital women of menopausal age in 1903: "The woman of fifty who only a few years ago would have been sent to the ranks of dowagers and grandmothers, today is celebrated for distinctive charm and beauty, ripe views, disciplined intellect, cultivated and manifold gifts." Once the Twenties got underway, however, the former stereotypes resurfaced.

The most famed women writers over the past hundred years have largely ignored, or been ignorant of, menopause. The romantic novels of George Sand, one of the most staggeringly prolific writers of the nineteenth century in the French language, were read as widely as Balzac's and Hugo's throughout the European continent. Sand also penned twenty-five volumes of letters while inspiring the music of her younger lover, Frederic Chopin. Yet in this vast landscape of words scholar Marilyn Yalom has uncovered only two personal letters in which Sand refers to the symptoms of menopause. In the first, written to her editor, Hetzel, in 1853, Sand was forty-nine years old:

> I am as well as I can be, given the crisis of my age. So far everything has taken place without grave consequence, but with sweats that I find overwhelming, and which are laughable because they are imaginary. I experience the phenomenon of believing that I am sweating 15 or 20 times a day and night . . . I have both the heat and the fatigue. I wipe my face with a white handkerchief and it is laughable because I am not sweating at all. However, that makes me very tired.

Sand was chiding herself out of ignorance for having hot flashes and night sweats. Often a woman does not perspire, even though she is experiencing an abrupt leap in skin temperature of one or two degrees. "Even today it's very difficult to explain to a woman that it's a real neurophysiological event, and therefore nothing she should be ashamed of," says Dr. Robert Lindsay, an endocrinologist and leading researcher in the field of menopausal medicine at the Helen Hayes Bone Center in West Haverstraw, New York. Not until the mid-1970s were laboratory tests developed that could demonstrate objectively the neurological discharge in the brain that causes the subjective changes women describe. When a woman says, "I am now having a hot flash," a machine similar to an EKG will show a spike in the ink line running across it.

George Sand refused to allow this inconvenience to interrupt her productivity and finished her letter by saying, "Nonetheless I am working and I've just done a play in three acts . . ." Weeks later she indicated in a letter to her son that she had "rounded the horn" and felt better than she had for a long time. Sand was smart enough to know that even she should make a healthy adaptation in the exhausting nocturnal work habits she had devised, as a young mother, to work around domestic duties. "I sleep well, I eat well, I no longer have those flashes and I'm working without fatigue. It is true that I don't give myself to excess anymore and at one o' clock in the morning I wrap myself in my bed without hesitation."

One in the morning, for George Sand, was early. After fifty she stopped writing from midnight to four A.M. But by then she was a polished professional with twenty years of writing behind her, and she was able to ensconce herself at her country estate and produce the many novels for which she is famous. George Sand was still vibrant, and still writing, when she died at the age of seventy-two.

Anais Nin, another fearless watchwoman over the back alleys of the female psyche, neglected the subject in her writings. Virginia Woolf's fragile nature was bedeviled by physical illness and mental anguish at every stage. She attracted particularly harsh criticism for the book that expressed her viewpoint as a woman in her fifties, *Three Guineas*. Woolf attributed none of her ills to menopause and never mentioned it in her writings, though she must have passed through it before she took her own life at fifty-nine. Colette was one of the rare writers to mention menopause at all in her work, portraying it in her novel *Break of Day* as both daunting and potentially empowering.

Fast-forward a hundred years and we find the same kind of fear and shame around hormonal changes—on the part of men! At least two recent American presidents have been on hormone replacement therapy. John Kennedy's adrenal glands were almost completely deteriorated. (Without the regulatory hormones the adrenals produce, wasting and death is the end result.) Even as he campaigned in the watershed 1960 election against Richard Nixon, Kennedy's hormonal condition was kept under control by replacement hormones. A wall of denial and cover stories kept his adrenal insufficiency and HRT regimen secret for many years, the silence being broken only in 1992 by two pathologists who had conducted the autopsy on President Kennedy.

Similarly, the public didn't know that George Bush had started hormone replacement therapy while he was president. He began acting jittery in the summer of 1991. The public puzzled over the manic energy he displayed, racing around in his cigarette boat and jumping from one sport to another, all the while he was calling together a worldwide military response to Saddam Hussein's invasion of Kuwait. The White House doctor eventually disclosed that the president's overactive thyroid gland had been treated with radioactive iodine and destroyed in April 1991 and that he had to take a daily dose of the hormone that his body no longer made naturally.

The thyroid hormone is a major regulator of the body's metabolism. Its functions can be easily maintained by taking the hormone, but the body is highly sensitive to dosages, and chronic stress or heavy travel with changing of time zones can throw everything off. Thus, when Bush began behaving erratically and making constant verbal gaffes in his speeches at the height of his summer 1992 reelection campaign, a wave of rumors about his health flooded the stock market. The crisis prompted his doctor, Burton Lee, to disclose to the press that he had recently been "messing around" with Bush's dosage of hormone replacement.

So, even world leaders can have volatile hormones.

Women Entering the Enlightened Age

$\mathcal{I}$s biology destiny? Of course not. But there are militant defenders of the opposing doctrine of "cultural determinism" who want us to believe that, beneath the learned male and female roles that culture lays upon us, all people are essentially similar. Understandably, there is strong resistance to believing that our behavior is influenced by the biochemical balance in our bodies, because it suggests that we have very little free will. It's unfortunate, and silly, to make it an either/or argument. If you ask me whether I believe in free will, I would borrow the answer given by Isaac Bashevis Singer: "Of course, I have no choice."

Any honest examination of the hormonal differences between women and men—or between women and other women, for that matter—is dismissed as a surrender to the old biology-as-destiny credo by writers like Barbara Ehrenreich. The cessation of menses, she wants us to believe, is "an obvious nonevent." (Like puberty, I suppose.) Menopause isn't an event at all, but a process that takes place over five to seven years and has as many profound metaphysical, social, and sexual layers of meaning as the passage of menarche, which ushers in a woman's fertility.

These polemicists seriously misrepresent the movement to bring menopause out of the closet. Beware of this logic when you encounter it. The proponents are often women frozen in an outdated era of feminism. Ignoring a host of new data that demonstrate some clear gender differences stemming, at least in part, from variations in male/female biology, they represent their views as a higher good than the truth. It can make them more dangerous than the wrong drug.

Animal studies have shown how fickle behavior can be, depending upon the amount of male or female hormone present in either sex. Strong evidence already exists connecting the aggressive behavior of males with the male hormone, testosterone. The more startling observations come from very recent studies of hyenas at the University of California, Berkeley. In the case of other animals, male babies engage in more rough play than females, due to the early testosterone they had circulating during fetal life. In a unique situation in all of biology, the hormonal bath in which female hyena fetuses grow is loaded with estrogen and testosterone, as well as androstenedione, a precursor able to be transformed into more fiery doses of testosterone. The females develop a huge clitoris at birth and eventually display a hanging genital that has erections and is indistinguishable from a male penis.

At the hyena pen in Berkeley, I watched the amazing gender-bending behavior that results from this biological switch. No sooner were they born than two females began tearing each other apart. When the third female of triplets emerged, she was barely an hour old before her sisters began chewing at her birth sack. The point was observable before our very eyes: high testosterone accounts for aggressive behavior in both males and females.

As they age, the female hyenas' level of testosterone dips

well below that of the males'. Notwithstanding, the females continue to be the more pugnacious and to remain in charge of their animal hierarchy. Dr. Lawrence Frank and Dr. Steven Glickman, animal behaviorists coordinating the study, tossed a huge hunk of horse meat into the pen of the young adults. The ranking female leapt on it and began reducing it to a grease spot, while the male lay back, passively, until she'd had her fill. "At this point, he defers to her without giving it a second thought," observed Dr. Glickman. By then, learned behavior has taken over from hormones. Thus does it remain difficult to disentangle culture from hormonal effects.

A clear link has been established, for example, between estrogen and women's verbal superiority, just as there is a link between testosterone and men's facility with math and visual-spatial tasks. The levels of hormone matter as well. When women of reproductive age were studied recently, their verbal dexterity was found to peak in the middle of their monthly cycle—just when estrogen levels were at their highest. Immediately after they finished menstruating, when circulating estrogen was at its lowest monthly ebb, their speed on verbal tasks declined. Even at their lowest speed, however, most of the women outperformed men on all verbal tests. By the same token, pubescent boys who have abnormally low levels of testosterone do poorly on spatial tasks.

In pulling together these recent studies, anthropologist Helen E. Fisher, author of *Anatomy of Love: The Natural History of Monogamy, Adultery, and Divorce*, proposes that these subtle gender differences make evolutionary sense. When ancestral males squatted in the African veldt to watch and hunt animals many millennia ago, those who were best in the visual-spatial skills of mapping and tracking might well have survived disproportionately. Similarly, ancestral women needed minute manual dexterity to pick seeds and berries out of the dense vegetation, while verbal skills may have been critical to communicating with their young; again, selecting for these traits in modern women.

"For decades, if not centuries, scientists in search of an understanding of human nature have used male behavior as a benchmark and compared all data on females with this standard," writes Fisher, pointing out this is why we have known almost nothing about the biological tendencies of women. Now that we are just beginning to learn, it would be a shame to throw out the baby with the ancestral bathwater. Fisher makes a good case from anthropological findings that the two sexes survived by teaming up and sharing one another's biological advantages. ". . . our ancestors had begun to collect, butcher, and share meat. The sexes had started to make their living as a team . . . this hunting-gathering lifestyle would produce an intricate balance between women, men, and power."

The question inevitably comes up, Is there a male menopause? Yes, but there are important differences. All men do not become infertile at around the same age, and some men continue to have sufficient testosterone to sire children well into older age. Nevertheless, according to leading endocrinologists I have consulted, a decline in sexual prowess is a clear phenomenon among men, and it is correlated with a decline in testosterone levels. Dr. Pentti Siiteri, former professor and codirector of the Reproductive Endocrinology Center at University of California, San Francisco, and an authority on hormonal mechanisms, explains, "This is analogous to what happens to a female, the significant difference being there is no sharp demarcation point; therefore, it is impossible to define when the decline in sexual prowess starts. Most men," he adds, "begin to taper off in their mid-fifties to sixties."

But they don't talk about it. Not to their wives. Not even to other men. "Because you don't want to admit weakening," adds Dr. Frank. "Your job as a male is to be strong."

"Sooner or later, however, virtually *all* men will have a male menopause," states Dr. Siiteri. "It's the difference between a gradual decline and a more abrupt one."

Now here's the good news for women. Biology at the Change of Life works to women's advantage. The turmoil wrought by menopause mixes up the hormonal cocktail in new and different proportions. As the levels of the primary female hormone, estrogen, continually decline, the chaser of male hormone, testosterone, increases in ratio. Before menopause, the average woman's level of testosterone is roughly 300 picograms. After a woman goes through the Change, if her ovaries are still intact, her testosterone level falls from 300 to about 215-220—or one-third. (If her ovaries are removed, the drop is to about 100, or a two-thirds fall). At the same time, her estrogen level falls twelve-fold, a far greater decrease than that in the male hormone. And after the Change, her estrogen level remains fairly constant.

Therefore, the balance between female and male hormones is dramatically altered by menopause. "In a premenopausal woman the ratio of testosterone to estrogen is roughly two to one, whereas in a *post*menopausal woman the ratio is roughly twenty to one," concludes Dr. Howard Judd, professor of Obstetrics and Gynecology at the University of California, Los Angeles (UCLA), whose scientific studies established these norms.

This provides a biological basis that would explain, at least in part, the widespread phenomenon of postmenopausal zest and the greater assertiveness recorded, cross-culturally, among postmenopausal women. Aggressiveness is rooted in the male hormone testosterone and found in elevated levels in men and male baboons of high rank.

Hence, in many societies, middle-aged women—freed from the role of breeder and fired up with relatively higher levels of testosterone—rise in rank and power, in political, religious, economic and community life. Margaret Mead, a mentor of mine, summed it up in one sentence: "There is no greater power in the world than the zest of a postmenopausal woman."

Indeed, the most powerful woman in the world throughout the decade of the Eighties was a menopausal woman. Margaret Thatcher was just about fifty when she broke the glass ceiling in British politics and became leader of the Conservative Party. She went through menopause while making the leap to world leader. Eleanor Roosevelt, Golda Meir, and Indira Gandhi all came into their own in their postmenopausal years.

Today, many more women are rising to high levels in public life in Europe and America, and without having to be honorary males. Among the 145 women in the European Parliament are some very glamorous ladies indeed. The British House of Commons now seats sixty-two women. The first woman to sit on the U.S. Supreme Court, Sandra Day O'Connor, and the first woman governor of Texas, the salty-tongued Ann Richards, are prime examples of strong-minded women with plenty of postmenopausal zest. Twenty-nine of the fifty-four political women who were elected to the U.S. Congress in 1992 were in their fifties or over. Across Europe and North America there seems to be a new recognition: You don't have to be old and gray and male to be knowledgeable. You can be fifty and female and fabulous.

It would be remiss of me to represent all contemporary women in their middle years as similarly enlightened. Indeed, some of those with readiest access to the facts of life about the postmenopausal years are the most confused by the politicized debate over HRT. Some bury their heads in the sand and refuse to know what they know, or do much about it.

Doctors Coming out of the Dark Ages

$\sim$

So often women say, "I'm waiting for my doctor to tell me what to do."

Lamentably, few doctors are well informed about menopause. Medical schools spend no more than a half day on the subject, if that, I am told by doctors themselves. Many doctors assume the vaguely described symptoms are psychological in nature. Since physicians are temperamentally disposed to helping people, they, too, feel frustrated at the state of scientific ignorance about women's health in the middle years.

"You don't need to know about that yet" is one standard answer women are given. The doctor pats her on the head, and out the door she goes with her migrainous headaches, ill-defined blues, or unexplained fatigue—What could it be? More commonly, she won't even bring up menopause, and her gynecologist won't either. Some women spend the next three to five years making the rounds of internists, neurologists, even psychiatrists, with no resolution, because they all ignore the obvious.

The experience of a busy professional political activist in

Washington is emblematic. Noticing her periods were scanty and intermittent and feeling uncharacteristically draggy, she went to her internist and plunked down three hundred dollars for a complete physical. She was forty-nine. The physician took a considerable amount of blood for tests. The results shed no light on her condition. Only when the activist talked to a woman friend who asked, "What about your estrogen level?" did the lightbulb flash on. She realized her doctor had not taken any hormone levels. He had never even mentioned menopause.

"The most important change going on in the body of a forty-nine-year-old woman was never addressed," she says, chagrined at her own passivity. "Doctors treat our bodies as though we're the same machines as men, and we're not."

A woman's own signs are her best guide as to whether or not she is nearing menopause or what phase of the long transition she might be in, and whether it is causing her problems. But in order to recognize those signs, and deal with each appropriately, *we must be educated*. It will not do to retreat behind the defense, *If I don't acknowledge it, it doesn't exist.*

Educated women have begun to let their doctors know they want a *dialogue* about menopause—a safe environment to ask questions and explore options—not to have hormones thrown at them. Physicians and medical centers have responded. Doctors (125,000 of whom are women today) are fighting over which specialty is best able to treat this newly identified and lucrative patient group. But one doctor can't know everything about all of the short- and long-term health issues involved in the biological and psychological transition of menopause. Women who have problems should be encouraged to seek help from different professionals if they need it, says Dr. Fredi Kronenberg, the director of menopause research at Columbia-Presbyterian Medical Center.

In 1991, then-NIH director Dr. Bernadine Healy marshaled the government's backing for the Women's Health Initiative (WHI). Now well under way, with women volunteering by the thousands, the largest clinical study of women's health in American history is investigating whether women who use artificial hormone therapy for many years are actually better-protected or at greater risk from such postmenopausal health hazards as heart disease, breast cancer, colon and rectal cancer, and fractures from osteoporosis. The earliest results will not be reported before the year 2000. Until then women and their physicians will have to make a compact to act as partners.

Some obstetrician-gynecologists find the menopausal woman an unappealing patient. She isn't going to have any more babies. Apart from a hysterectomy, there is little chance she will require surgery—the moneymaking part of the practice—but she can be expected to complain about vague symptoms and ask questions for which even a sympathetic physician has only unsatisfactory answers. With candor, a dedicated female gynecologist describes the attitudes of many of her male colleagues: "They find us tedious because we're going to take up their time, and threatening because we're smart and we're grown-ups—we don't want any of their bullshit."

This is not to imply that all male gynecologists are dismissive or that all female gynecologists are sympathetic. Women who have felt the necessity to deny their femaleness in order to "pass" in male-dominated medical schools and hospital settings may disassociate from menopause entirely, and they can be quite brutal with women patients who bring them a grab bag of complaints.

The busy doctor of either sex is likely to take an incomplete family history of the factors that impinge on menopause. Just how cursory these conversations can be is illustrated by the experience of a well-known columnist and her sister, both hard on age fifty. They consulted the same gynecologist in the Boston area to ask what to do.

Despite their genetic likeness, one was told she was a good candidate for hormones. Her sister was cautioned not to take hormones. It turns out that the sisters had emphasized different subjective fears. Representative Patricia Schroeder of Colorado, active in the campaign for women's health research and funding, cracks that "If you get six menopausal women together, you'll find that their doctors are doing six different things. Our joke is that you might as well go to a veterinarian."

Dr. Mathilde Krim, the indefatigable AIDS activist and former pioneer in interferon research, relates another typical story. "Very early on in my life I was shocked by the great indifference of male doctors to the health problems particular to women," she says, recalling the unnecessary secondary suffering of a woman cancer patient at Memorial Sloan-Kettering Cancer Center. Dr. Krim had been called into the group of male physicians discussing the woman's case: Her cancer was of the lung. The patient was asked what other medications she took. "Estrogen," she volunteered.

"That's the first thing to cut out," the men ordered.

"Why, if it makes her feel better?" demanded Dr. Krim. "It was absurd. The poor woman had all these problems with her lung cancer, and now she had to suffer hot flashes on top of it." But the male physicians were gratuitously adamant. And of course, the patient did not dare to raise a complaint.

There is a simple blood test a woman can ask for that is quite reliable in determining whether or not, and at what stage, she is in menopause. One should ask to have one's LH and FSH measured, along with the level of estrogen. FSH, a follicle-stimulating hormone, and LH, a luteinizing hormone, are responsible for ovulation and under the control of the hormones estrogen and progesterone. If the FSH and LH are both high, in the presence of low estrogen, it is indicative of menopause.

The Hysterectomy Trap

~

$\mathscr{H}$ysterectomies are the second most common surgery for women in America, where proliferation in this surgery is more than double the rate in most European countries. It is not even known exactly how many hysterectomies are performed on women each year in the U.S., because there is no organization that keeps national statistics on hysterectomies. In fact, the National Center for Health Statistics does not have a department that deals specifically with gynecological issues. But the generally accepted estimate is that one out of three American women will surrender her womb to the surgeon's knife—usually between the ages of twenty-five and forty-four.

A mere 11 percent of the surgical menopause surgeries performed in the U.S. are done in response to a cancerous growth. Notwithstanding, some gynecologists urge women to consider a "prophylactic hysterectomy"; that is, to undergo major surgery on the chance that at some future time she might develop cancer in her reproductive organs. A stylish ob-gyn man in Beverly Hills recommends prophylactic hysterectomies along with removal of the ovaries when his patients reach menopause.

A Seattle divorcée brags about solving the whole dilemma by having just such an elective hysterectomy at the age of forty-one. "My doctor was a yanker instead of a saver," she quips. "But I wasn't going to use the equipment anymore, I didn't want it. I'm glad I got rid of my ovaries."

It may sound like a nice midlife housecleaning, but that brings us to another myth about the Change: If you have a hysterectomy, you bypass menopause. A case in point is the story of a Rochester woman I interviewed, a college professor in the social sciences. Virginia, who requested anonymity, was seen by her family and friends and colleagues as a super-coper. At the age of forty-seven, she separated from her husband. She went into perimenopause at the same time, but she didn't know it.

"I was agitated all the time," she recalls, looking back. "I thought I was losing my memory. I had night sweats and blurred vision. Sometimes I'd be so fatigued, coming home from school, my legs would fold underneath me climbing up the stairs."

And then came the all-too-common admission: "I thought, because I'd had a hysterectomy, I wouldn't have a menopause." Virginia never asked her doctor. And her doctor, a woman GP, said nothing to enlighten her. So, how did she manage?

Virginia would get into her car after work, two or three times a week, and drive an hour and a half to Buffalo. There, unrecognized, invisible, she could sit in a shopping mall and cry.

"I was like two people," she recalls with anguish. Back home again, she would get strokes for being a super-coper. Only recently, in Virginia's fifty-second year, her doctor finally did blood tests to measure her hormone levels, and announced: "Virginia, you're finished with menopause."

It was the first time the subject had come up.

If both a woman's ovaries are removed, she will go into instant menopause. It is actually castration. Twice as many women who have a hysterectomy today, compared to twenty years ago, also have their ovaries removed. For a woman with a persistent ovarian tumor, it is common and necessary to have at least one ovary removed. However, before having both ovaries removed, a woman should be warned that the abrupt and total, rather than gradual, shutting down of ovarian function can be devastating, placing her at risk of serious depression. It also extinguishes sexual desire. Unless a woman immediately starts hormone replacement therapy and commits to remaining on the medication indefinitely, she will have all the symptoms of menopause, whatever her age. What's more, early surgical removal of the ovaries *doubles* the risk of osteoporosis. If you lose your ovaries at age thirty, by the time you reach age fifty, your *bone age* may be seventy. Yet doctors often neglect to warn a woman that the surgery can have such lifelong effects even after the body heals.

I ran into this same high-handed attitude in a heavily utilized menopause clinic in the heart of London. When women complain about side effects from progesterone drugs, this doctor, like many, will often recommend a hysterectomy. He explains that it will free them from having to take the progesterone to protect their uterus. I asked if he would routinely take the ovaries as well?

"In a postmenopausal woman, the ovaries are of no use anyway," he replied dismissively. I expressed alarm. Wasn't this extreme? The doctor was ignoring the fact that the ovaries continue to produce testosterone, which strongly influences a woman's sexual desire and energy.

"To a lot of people that seems like using a sledgehammer to open a nut," he granted. "But for patients who suffer badly, and desperately want to continue their HRT—especially women in their early-to-middle-forties who are faced with this for another ten years—they say, 'God, I can't take these side effects anymore, take it all away.'" He boasted that all such women, convinced by him to go ahead with a hysterectomy, "thought it was the best thing since sliced bread."

How much did he question women about their sexual pleasure and comfort, a year after performing these hysterectomies? I inquired.

"I must admit, personally speaking, not a great deal," the surgeon said. "Mrs. Smith comes in, has a hysterectomy, you see her six or eight weeks later, and if she's making a satisfactory recovery, you don't see her again."

"The concept that the ovary burns out is not true," claims one of the experts on the postmenopausal ovary, Dr. Howard Judd at UCLA. Although a woman's ovaries stop producing estrogen, in postmenopause they continue to produce a significant amount of testosterone. A study that did take the trouble to consider the impact on sex life following a hysterectomy found that between 33 and 46 percent of the women whose ovaries had also been removed complained of reduced sexual responsiveness.

Fibroids often lead women to unnecessary hysterectomies. These benign growths are found in 20 percent of all women. (Fibroids are far more common among African-American women than white women, according to the National Black Women's Health Project.) Although the popularity of hysterectomy is highest in the South—"Mississippi appendectomy" it's called—and lowest in the Northeast, where statistically there are more educated women, it is very common for women to mistake the normal symptoms of perimenopause for a more serious problem. Here is a typical scenario from the Massachusetts Women's Health Study of twenty-five thousand women, aged forty-five to fifty-five, from all socioeconomic levels:

A woman who is perimenopausal but doesn't know it goes to her doctor to report heavy bleeding. "Is this the Change?" she asks. He tells her she's too young for the

Change, but she'd better have a D&C. The study investigators follow up eighteen months later. By now, the woman has gone in for two or three D&C's, which haven't stopped the bleeding because it wasn't caused by abnormal pathology. It was normal perimenopause. But by now the woman is so scared, she ends up having a hysterectomy.

Now, what could this woman have done instead? A simple office biopsy of the lining of the uterus may document any evidence of premalignant changes. Or, she could have a hysteroscopy, an examination that allows the physician to look inside the cavity of the uterus and see if there is a polyp or fibroid. If there is still doubt, she could take a three-month course of hormone replacement, to see if the dysfunctional bleeding is resolved.

There are now drugs that can be taken to treat some conditions that would otherwise lead to hysterectomy. After drugs have shrunk the fibroids, if necessary, they can be removed by laparoscopy or by a technique known as myomectomy.

Some women with fibroid tumors do have clear indicators for hysterectomy: first, rapid growth of the tumor that may be a sign of cancer developing in the fibroid; second, uncontrollable bleeding; third, fibroid size so large that other organs may be compromised; or, finally, intractable pain.

More and more, educated women are beginning to see themselves as selective consumers of health care and refusing to accept any doctor's word as oracular. And when they find out how little the doctors know, or anybody knows, about this oldest of female physical transitions, they are mad as hell.

The TV producer mentioned earlier who suffered embarrassment with hot flashes at a dinner party is a case in point. When she reported her problem to her gynecologist, he said, noticeably bored, "Oh, yeah, fifty years old, you're right on target. Menopause."

"What can I do about it?" inquired the take-charge producer, accustomed to handling an eight-million-dollar budget.

"You just start taking estrogen."

She asked what were the implications of taking hormones.

"Well, you'll have to go for a breast X-ray twice a year instead of once a year. But there's no risk."

"If there's no risk, then why do I have to go twice as often?" she replied, thinking logically. He brushed off her question with a few remarks that sounded like he was reading out of a manual: *How to Handle the Over-the-Hill Patient.*

"That made me defiant," says the producer. Finally she insisted he tell her if there was anything that would treat the hot flashes. He told her about the old standby called Bellergal. He warned, "But that won't help with irritability, depression, crying—all the rest of it."

"Maybe I won't have any 'rest of it,'" the producer said, her adrenaline pumping full strength. "In the meantime, so I don't have to spend the next ten years in a terrycloth robe, I'll try the Bellergal." She got up to leave.

"You can do that," said the gynecologist, with what she read as an arrogant smirk. "But you'll be back."

The normal preamble to menopause is sometimes treated with a casualness bordering on the criminal. "This uterus looks a little bit tired," a male gynecologist told a forty-year-old North Carolina woman, "guess we'll take her out." It was typical of the attitude among some doctors that the uterus is little more than a nuisance. Since this patient was a housekeeper, without all the fancy scientific words to defend the tired "her," all she could do was "fight to keep my uterus."

At a higher status level, another Southern woman, a fifty-three-year-old graduate student I will call Katherine, ran into a more subtle insensitivity from her male gynecologist and her male internist. Katherine had spent fifty years doing what she was "supposed" to do: fitting her life into the interstices of her children's and husband's lives. Once her children were well launched, Katherine felt a deep need to be "credentialed" as a professional. "But we're out of sync with the family life cycle," she observed. Determined to make up for lost time, she became accustomed to working seventeen hours a day to get her master's degree and apply for a doctoral program.

"Suddenly, at fifty, I could barely function. I couldn't write a paper after four in the afternoon, but all my complaints were vague," she confessed. "Neither doctor would give me hormones. All they know is I'm not *supposed* to be trying to get my doctorate at fifty-three. Why don't I just go home and calm down?"

At some level we *know* when the Change begins to come upon us. The sense of unease or disequilibrium is something women feel, though it remains incomprehensible to those who have not experienced it. Isn't it amazing that women should allow organized medicine, filtered through a male perspective, to tell us how we feel? (How many men know what it's like to be one week late? Or two weeks early while you're teaching a class in a white suit?) Medical breakthroughs in this century have given us the gift of greatly extended life spans; now attention should be turned to bringing *healthier* life spans. And that means women must become informed, active consumers of good health care. But because up to the present day we have accepted a way of thinking that denies or denigrates this epic change in our bodies and the exciting new vistas it can open in our minds, we have failed to demand that decent scientific research be done.

Our tax dollars have supported massive research on heart disease among men (while leaving women out of those clinical trials entirely), but our national health institutes cannot give us any definitive data about the long-term impact of the body's postreproductive state on women's health. The National Institutes of Health has spared only 13 percent of its revenues to study women's health. If you compare the level of our scientific knowledge about the causes and effects of menopause with the evolution of modern medicine, it is as though bacteria has not been discovered yet and we were still dependent on leeches and roots and shamans to cure what ails us.

Medical schools still use terms such as *the weeping of the uterus* to describe menstruation, assigning emotions to a bodily organ because it wasn't fertilized by male sperm that month. The classical medical terminology for menopause is *ovarian failure*.

Another way of seeing it would be as *ovarian fulfillment*. One has put in thirty or forty years of ripening eggs and enduring the hormonal mischief of monthly cycles, on the chance that a child is wanted. Enough, say most women in middle age. We're ready to move on now, to find our place in the world, free of the responsibilities of our procreative years. It's time to take risks and pursue passions and allow ourselves adventures perhaps set aside way back at thirteen, when we accepted the cultural script for our gender that ordinarily denied those dreams. It's time to play! And kick up some dust!

Cinderella Hits
Menopause

~

$\mathcal{A}$s the pacesetters among baby boom generation women discover menopause on their horizon, they are bringing it out of the closet. This has been happening only in the last few years. Even the earliest conversations in a previous generation would have been unimaginable.

I went to Los Angeles in 1991 to join in such conversations. It seemed that my article had stirred up a little *frisson* of fright among some of the movers and shakers in the film community. In that world, where leading ladies never look a day over twenty-nine and studio executives start subtracting years from their résumés before they hit thirty, Hollywood producer Lynda Guber had picked up a copy of *Vanity Fair* and discovered a cloud on the horizon of her perfect existence.

"Menopause!" she shrieked. "God, I've never seen that word written."

Lynda is a sizzling redhead from Brooklyn who has reached the pinnacle of Hollywood society together with her husband, Peter Guber, producer of *Batman* and *Rainman*, former head of SONY Pictures Entertainment, and now head of his own production company. The next day she bumped into Joanna Poitier at a Beverly Hills bistro and asked innocently, "How are you doing?"

"I'm a lunatic; I'm going through menopause and empty nest at the same time," said the beautiful actress-wife of actor Sidney Poitier. (It is culture-specific to Hollywood to identify women by their husbands' professional status.)

This is fantastic, thought Lynda. *This woman is ready to talk about how she feels.* Lynda herself had already decided "the impact of menopause will not be devastating on me, that's what my holistic belief system tells me," but all she knew about it, in fact, was that the subject was a real no-no. Lynda is committed to being a consciousness-raiser of people in the movie business, having cofounded an organization, Education 1st!, that spreads positive messages through TV shows. She passed the word to a friend, Annie Gilbar, then editor of *LA Style.* "Annie, I have an idea. I'd like to have a meeting on menopause with the girls." The first invitees backed off. But word spread, and before long it became such a cachet event, there had to be a luncheon and a dinner group. I was invited to come out and speak to both. My friend and gynecologist, Dr. Patricia Allen, accompanied me.

Going to Hollywood to talk about menopause was a little bit like going to Las Vegas to sell savings accounts. Such is the obsession with youthfulness in Southern California, one half expects there to be an ordinance against menopause there. "Women who are menopausal in California are around the bend—they view it like cancer," I was warned by a Chinese medicine specialist with a deluxe and desperate clientele in Los Angeles.

Nevertheless, it was a golden opportunity. California women in the boomer vanguard are normally the most uninhibited among their species in speaking out about whatever bothers them. I quickly discovered, however, that even they—women who have access to the most up-to-date information, women who are religious about doing the stations of their Nautilus machines, women who have phone indexes with the names of dozens of doctors, not to mention the best acupuncturists, herbalists, liposuctionists, and shrinks—even they didn't have any answers on menopause. In fact, they had never discussed the questions, even among themselves. When they did come together to confront the subject, they reflected many of the secret fears and defensive reactions common among women everywhere.

Lynda invited us to gather at her Japanese-style fantasy beach house. At the door each woman was invited to leave her shoes on a shelf and choose a kimono. I kept looking for a gray hair in the crowd—scarcely a one among this mostly blond, mid-fortyish group. The guests draped themselves over big black cushions on tansu boxes in the screening room. It was reminiscent of slumber parties in junior high school, when girls played dress-up and talked about taboo subjects like sex. But now we were grown-ups; and the very fact these prominent women had shown up, in this subculture, was an act of bravery.

"I invited Glenn Close to come," said one of the women. "I thought she was going to faint dead away."

I began by asking those present to introduce themselves, give their age, and say why they had come—what meaning did menopause have for them? The wife of one of the town's top studio executives confessed she usually shunned "negative subjects," but her mother was dead and she had no one else to consult. A woman who heads her own company described herself as an information junkie. "My gynecologist tells me that I'm not going through the Change at all, but I know my body, and I feel different over the past year. I've had occasional night sweats. I used to think I had a virus."

Lisa Specht, a lawyer, has no children and said she didn't think she had to worry about menopause, at least until she was fifty-five or something. "I haven't had any symptoms yet, except that my skin has been oily," she assured herself.

The outspoken Joanna Poitier broke the ice. She was willing to admit she might be going through menopause, although her primary concern was letting go of her two daughters, now eighteen and twenty. "I keep waking up in the middle of the night, changing my nightgown. I went to the gynecologist, and she told me that I was still moist. She said I won't probably go into menopause for another two years. I have night sweats. I tried it without the duvet and the nightgown, and I still have night sweats. I have day sweats, too! The back of my neck is damp all day long."

The next speaker was immediately recognizable. Lesley Ann Warren, the movie actress we all remember from her ethereal portrayal of Cinderella in the TV musical, is even more beautiful today. Her features are still delicate, her body is still slim and supple, and reddish brown hair ripples over her shoulders. More appealing than all that are the quickened intelligence and candor that she has earned over forty years and has brought to her more recent roles in the films *Victor/Victoria* and *Choose Me*. But Lesley Ann makes her living here in Cinderella Land, where girls are never supposed to grow up. Hollywood ruthlessly cuts the finest actresses once they reach forty—yes, even Meryl! Studio executives will callously describe a thirty-eight-year-old actress who is still gorgeous as "over the hill" or "She's an old hag." As an actress in that workplace, Lesley Ann Warren is torn between her liberated feminist beliefs and the devastating reality that every day her worth is judged by her age and her looks.

Divorced from Jon Peters, former cohead of the former Columbia Studios, with whom she had a son, Lesley Ann had been single for some time. She now had a new love. It was he who found a photocopy of my *Vanity Fair* article lying around. Lesley Ann wanted to educate herself on the subject before it happened so she could deal with it homeopathically and herbally, as she does everything else. She had forgotten to hide the evidence.

"You know, I read this article," he said casually one night.

Ohmigod, he's found me out! was the actress's first thought. "I was really scared he would think *I* was menopausal. I felt ashamed." But he surprised her.

"I'm glad I read it. I feel like any man who's in a relationship with a woman dealing with this must be very loving, very aware, and very present," he said.

Lesley Ann counted her new love among an ultramicroscopic subspecies of the male genus, at least as they are bred by the movie business. "In all the rest of my experience, men are so staggeringly uneducated in this area, it's deadly for us," she told the group. "Most men I know run from the word *menopause.*"

"We're afraid to educate the men, that's our problem," amended Joanna. "I have never been afraid to say how old I am. I've never had surgery or collagen or anything like that. And I don't feel any less terrific because I'm menopausal. Whoever you are with, they should experience the whole thing that you're experiencing." Joanna added vociferously, "I take no aspirin, no Tylenol; if I have a headache, I live through it. I don't believe in pills. I know that I will not take hormones, because to me it's unnatural."

The word *holistic* was almost a fetish in this group. Used indiscriminately, it might mean one who never uses Tylenol, or one who has stopped taking drugs and alcohol, or one who consults Chinese medical doctors and herbalists but never a member of the American Medical Association. A bouncy talent agent with a blond boy-cut admitted she was taking hormones; *admitted*, because, like so many women, her decision was tinged with guilt. "I knew something was up when I went to a restaurant and had to ask the waiter for two menus—one to see what I was ordering and the other to fan myself."

Knowing laughter rippled through the group. We decided that if we met again we would call ourselves The Fan Club.

The agent revealed a more intimate reason for her decision. "One night when my husband and I were having sex, it felt like I was a virgin. I said, 'Something is wrong here.' My gynecologist took a blood test and told me it was the Change of Life." She emphasized that she was on a very low dose of hormone replacement therapy and that she was happy with the results.

Joanna Poitier broke in with a question on everybody's mind. "Is it okay to go through the rest of life without estrogen?"

Dr. Allen said there was no definitive answer. "When we are in this part of our lives, we have to make decisions about what it is that we want. Beyond the symptomatic discomforts, there are also medical issues that bear on our long-term health—osteoporosis, heart disease, breast and uterine cancer." Dr. Allen's advice was to gather as much information as possible, including that concerning one's own family history, to find out if there is a medical reason to take hormone replacement therapy, and then make a decision.

"But we don't have to make a decision for life. We make a decision for three months, and then we make a decision again," she added, sowing visible relief in some of the tense faces. Others were impatient with this answer. They had come looking for a risk-free, all-natural curative.

Mary Miccuci introduced herself as a "stress queen." A tall, Cher-like streak of a woman who started her own catering business, Along Came Mary, she dashes around Hollywood putting on spreads for the stars. Her signs of menopause began with palpitations; she thought she was having a heart attack. "The quality of my life is changing—all of our lives are changing. I want information!" she said angrily, pitching forward to lean her elbows on her knees. "I want to go through this process as quickly as possible. I'm on a holistic journey to deal with it. Are there the right herbs to take care of the silent killers—heart disease and osteoporosis?"

Surely what they all wanted to hear from me and Dr. Allen was that some magic regimen—yoga and yogurt, or yams and ginseng and green leafy vegetables—would allow them to remain exactly as they had been: youthful wives, sexually appealing and responsive lovers, efficient career builders. They were not yet ready to consider a new self-definition. And until one is ready, the information that is available is not much use.

"I think that we have all been too passive about what the outcome of our lives should be," Mary continued huffily. "Because I tell you, the way I felt for a year was pretty shitty. I have a five-and-half-year-old little girl, and I want to be so together for this kid. This menopause stuff, I'll be god-damned if I'll let it get in my way."

Mary's hostility toward the whole subject was revelatory. She had become used to managing her life like a man, according to goals, timetables, balance sheets. She is a businesswoman accustomed to efficiency; in fact, she had to leave early to cater a screening party for Bette Midler's latest film. But now, at the peak of her productivity, she is feeling violated by this reassertion of her body's biologic identity. There is nothing efficient about "this menopause stuff."

Aloma Ichinose, a photographer equally active in her career, had taken the opposite approach. "I'm going through the Change right now. I feel great about it. But at first it was a nightmare. I was raised by a man, so none of this was ever talked about." Allowing time for trial and error, Aloma had made several different decisions over the previous year. When urine and blood tests confirmed that she was in menopause, her doctor put her on Premarin. To her, it felt like doing drugs. "I did the Premarin for six months. I felt wonderful, and all my symptoms—the disrupted sleep, the forgetfulness—went away." She added defensively, "I'm not into drugs. I haven't had a drink in years. But I was really worried about bone loss. I'm active, I'm a photographer, I need my strength." Eventually the fear and guilt over taking hormones got to her, and after the six months she stopped. "And all the symptoms returned," she admitted. "I just didn't feel well, and so I'm back on it again and I feel good."

An art gallery owner pressed the issue of age prevention. "How long do you take this? Will it prolong our youth? We are young in our forties, where people of other generations weren't. I'm forty-seven years old, but I don't think that I am forty-seven in numbers. I have the same energy as always."

Joanna, whose blond tendrils and soft curves help her to maintain the jolly all-American-girl good looks of a perpetual cheerleader, is able to maintain the illusion of her inner eye: "I still feel like I'm twenty-eight. I wear my hair the same way, I'm twenty-eight years old."

Another woman in the room muttered, "But you're not. And they know you're not."

It cut like a flesh wound into the self-image of every woman there. They were all attractive, and that statement didn't even need the qualifying prefix *still*. External beauty wasn't the real problem. It was the dysynchrony between their idealized inner images—the women they were at their nubile peaks—and blanks where the faces and bodies and spirits of their future selves would have to be filled in, sooner or later. As vanguard baby boomers, they agreed, they belonged to the most pampered, narcissistic and obstinately adolescent generation in American history. "We have delayed duty, responsibility, and commitment," wrote a spokeswomen for their generation, Lynn Smith, in the *Los Angeles Times*. "We have dieted, jogged, and exercised so much, we look and actually *think* we are five to ten years younger than we are."

The most telling reaction of all came from a sleek-looking South African woman who had been mute all night. Before I left, she took me aside and asked the quintessential Southern California question:

"Tell me, what can I do so I *don't have to have this?*"

Boomers' Gift to Women

*A*s a woman looks ahead to the Change, it is natural to focus entirely on the loss of powers one has taken for granted in previous stages. The youthful looks you could always trade on, and the magical powers of procreation that connected you to the cycle of all life—these are the God-given, gloriously unfair advantages of being born a well-formed woman. Suddenly, in the mid-forties, one must face the fact that these powers are ebbing. What will replace them?

The women who attended the luncheon meeting in Beverly Hills were ready to confront such issues. They were a mix of professionals who had left a mark on their respective fields: A top state politician, a mayor, and a judge were interspersed with well-known screenwriters, entertainment producers, and social activists. All but three of those present were in their mid-forties with still-young children.

"So many of us know each other," Annie Gilbar kept remarking, "and we talk about a lot of things—children, sex, everything—but this subject has never come up. Not once." Two of the creative talents in today's film industry were among the group: Meg Kasdan, coscreenwriter with husband Lawrence Kasdan of *Grand Canyon*, and executive producer Carole Isenberg (*The Color Purple* and *This Is My Life*). Both were flabbergasted when they couldn't think of a single reference in a film to a woman going through the Change and the impact it had on her life. "I'm always sneaking messages in about women's lives, but never this," said Carole. "It's a sorry statement that shows how unwilling and uncomfortable we have been to deal with this issue." Meg added, "Mature women—that is, over forty—are almost invisible in Hollywood movies."

One refreshing exception was the movie *Fried Green Tomatoes*, in which a miserable, menopausal Kathy Bates bounces off the walls until she has a heart-to-heart with the wise older woman played by Jessica Tandy. "Oh, Mrs. Threadgoode, I'm too young to be old and too old to be young. I just don't fit anywhere. I wish I could kill myself, but I don't have the courage."

Mrs. Threadgoode is appalled. "Why, Evelyn Couch, you mustn't even think such a thing. . . . You're just going through a bad case of menopause, that's all that's the matter with you. What you need is to take your hormones and to get out every day and walk in the fresh air and walk yourself right through it. That's what I did when I was in it. I used to burst into tears eating a steak, just thinkin' about that poor cow."

At the luncheon meeting, once people began to talk about menopause as more than a matter of spigots and pipes and secretions involving our organs, an important issue surfaced. Losing the magic—that was the deeper mutation to be accepted. The graduation from our fertile years resonates in our psyches as deeply as the squirm and throb in the belly of our first pregnancy signifies our awesome powers of creation. Like most graduations, it is the occasion for both relief and sadness.

"For many of us who waited until we were well into our thirties and even early forties before having children, the physical power of giving birth is still palpable; it touches something very deep and instinctual," ventured Suzanne Rosenblatt Buhai, a psychotherapist. "That flame of the instinctual being extinguished is not as readily dealt with as one might think."

Dealing with loss is one of the tasks we struggle with in every passage, but it is particularly poignant as women notice the first skips in a fertility we have probably taken for granted. The feelings were brought out by a woman who has obviously delighted in maternity. Joyce Bogart Trabulus has two children and a quartet of stepchildren in her life, and is further fulfilled by community caretaking in the form of running charities for cancer and AIDS research. She has no desire to have any more children. No *daylight world* desire.

"And yet I really feel sadness every time I think about it," Joyce admitted. "I was forty-one when I had my last child, who's three years old now—I almost feel like a grandmother to my own kid. And I sometimes catch myself thinking, *Oh God, this is fabulous, I'd love to do this again.* It's a great loss to know that it will be impossible for me. It's not like I want another one. And I'm not menopausal, or even premenopausal. But I look at a baby and say, 'Oh.' "

Suzanne mused out loud, "Given our generational narcissism—whether it's because of our sheer numbers, Dr. Spock, or the dominant influence of psychoanalysis—I just wonder if this concern with self is now being focused on menopause. Are we getting all worked up over something that is, in fact, quite normal and has been experienced since time immemorial? Perhaps the best gift we can give society at this stage is to see this as something very positive. If we can normalize this experience, as Gail says, it will help women deal with it. Otherwise, women will take on the responsibility of this somehow being their fault—they are supposed to be pulling out of this funk."

One of the few women in the room over fifty, Vicki Reynolds, then-mayor of Beverly Hills, looked around the group with eagerness and some envy. "I am almost a generation ahead of most of you," she said. "I have seen women my age go through menopause without the benefit of any medical enlightenment—ignorant of all you have been saying. Now we look to you, the baby boom generation, to talk about this openly and explore the effects and benefits of menopause. That's so exciting."

It was agreed that the vestigial attitude surrounding menopause—"I'm no good anymore"—would be changed by the way women like themselves handled it. I suggested, only half seriously, "If every woman in menopause told five people in the next week, those five people would have an entirely different view of it. 'This dish is in menopause? Well, maybe it isn't so terrible.'" Dr. Allen observed that at this stage we have responsibilities to the world, not just to our tiny communities. She is excited every day by finding new channels to educate women about their bodies. "That's my public passion," she said. "But we also need something for ourselves—new passions all the time."

I added wickedly, "And they may include a twenty-five-year-old lover."

"Yeah, a *blind* twenty-five-year-old lover!" amended one of the California women.

With a whooping and shimmying of laughter, the session ended. Seventeen women went out into the world to resume their balancing acts among careers, husbands, children, car pools, social and spiritual lives, too busy to worry much about menopause, but better prepared for the future. Laughter and forgetting . . . two of the best gifts women of any age can share with one another.

But something hopeful, something even incendiary had come out of those two sessions with California women. Their need to know was beginning to overcome their fear of knowing. Two years later, in 1994, I was asked by the women guests at Rancho la Puerta, a health spa in Baja, California, to give a talk on menopause. The atmosphere was totally different. The women were well-informed, unabashed, confident about asking sophisticated questions and offering smart alternatives from their own experience. And there were men in the group, empathetic husbands and savvy physicians. And we had a lot of laughs! It convinced me that the pacesetting women of this generation will shift the boundaries as well as the meaning of menopause: They will redefine it, and *live it*, as a midlife experience of minor importance in the scheme of a long and lushly various life.

The "What About Me?" Syndrome

~

*L*ess privileged women assume that menopause is just another burden of being a woman and simply bear it, though not grinning. But the class differences are glaring. The population tapped for the rare studies has been almost exclusively white, well educated, and motivated to take care of its health preventively. The vast majority of women in lower socioeconomic groups have no idea of the long-term health issues related to "the Change." They are so accustomed to bleeding and having cramps and premenstrual tension that when they hit menopause they just shrug and say, "Here we go again—male doctors treating me like I don't matter a damn."

That was Kate McNally's first reaction. A secretarial assistant in local government in a medium-size Long Island town, she was then fifty-five. All her life Kate had been a great coper, having had four children close together and launched them all as young adults of whom she can be proud. Her reward? "The most frustrating phase I've ever been through in my life—it's horrendous! I've never felt so helpless. Nobody understands menopause. And nobody knows what to do about it."

Kate went to her gynecologist complaining of heavy bleeding. After a questionable Pap smear, a cone biopsy was done, followed by a D&C. She was put on estrogen and told to have a mammogram. The results weren't conveyed to her for two months. A lump had been found. Of course, at first she blamed the hormones. But the great majority of breast tumors, including hers, are slow-growing. Her disease had probably been developing, undetected, for several years. The irony is, many women do not bother with a mammogram until they consult a doctor about indications of menopause. If a tumor is found, the culprit may look like hormones, but is probably the result of more careful medical surveillance.

After two lumpectomies, Kate was taken off estrogen forever. She was bedeviled by menopausal symptoms no one could tell her how to relieve. "I feel betrayed," she said softly. "I've always put others before myself. By this age I have more money to work with and more leisure time with the kids gone. I should have the energy to do the things I've always wanted." I asked what things she had looked forward to.

"Getting a decent night's sleep." This modest expectation was betrayed by the dull film over her blue eyes. "You go for years with little babies waking you up all night. Then the teen years when you can't sleep for worrying because they're out in your car. And now I'm the one awake all night!" She laughed hard. Her husband seemed wonderfully supportive, and Kate was determined to cope with this stage as she had with other trials in the past.

A treatment alternative for women like Kate might be tamoxifen, an estrogenlike drug that is protective of the heart and prevents bone loss at the same time as it protects the breasts against cancer. There are a number of tamoxifen trials under way around the country. Tamoxifen is not a perfect alternative since it does increase the risk of uterine cancer, but periodic examinations to check for changes in the uterus would detect this type of cancer, which is highly curable when found early.

Kate's sister, Bindy, was only forty-two and very attractive, with long, curly red hair and a sugar-doughnut figure wrapped in shorts and a T-shirt, but already she was wrestling with the emotional preamble to menopause. "I used to be the no-worry type. Just leave the house, go to the beach—nothing ever bothered me," she said. "I lost my temper but once in a blue moon." Suddenly she was a virtual powder keg. When her son didn't come to the table until his dinner was cold, she jumped up in such a childish rage she knocked over a chair. "Everybody looked at me as if I had three heads."

She told her girlfriend later, "They measured the chemicals in my brain with a blood test. They said the chemicals were out of balance and that indicated I was in menopause."

"That explains why you're so moody," sympathized her friend.

"Moody! I'm not moody!" Bindy remembers shrieking. "How can you say that? You're my best friend!"

These powerful hormones do, in fact, cross the blood-brain barrier. Sensors in the brain that control emotions pick up a signal when there is an erratic production of either estrogen or progesterone. In a person whose nervous system is finely tuned, these sensors overreact, triggering brain-chemistry changes and emotional symptoms. Veteran gynecologists affirm that some women can have physical symptoms from even slight changes in the amount of estrogen produced.

Every morning, as a waitress in a busy coffee shop, Bindy has to stroke hundreds of people who haven't had coffee yet. "The doctor told me to stop smoking, cut down on cholesterol, and avoid stress. Hah, avoid stress! How?"

She knows she is being grouchy and impossible. "But I

can't control it. And I'm afraid if I take this estrogen, then I'll have lumps like my sister."

Women like Kate and Bindy are often caught in the middle between caring for aging, fragile parents and dealing with the lingering financial dependence of children. Many experience the "What about me?" syndrome. They are not accustomed to nurturing themselves. But even as they are encouraged by books like this to pamper themselves through this transition, Western society is making more demands on them today than ever. Most middle-aged Americans today still have living parents, a change in family dynamics with no precedent in history. With many more people in the U.S. and Europe living into their eighties and nineties, and fewer children per family, geriatric research-ers warn that almost every woman is going to have to take care of an aging parent or parent-in-law.

That will put more and more women on the "daughter track," possibly for a decade or more, just as they are emerging from the "mommy track." Traditionally, it has been middle-aged women who are depended upon to do the work of unpaid caregiving for the disabled elderly at home. But women now also fill nearly half the paid positions *outside* the home. At just the stage when they expect to enter the most focused and productive period of their working lives, with their children grown and gone, they may not be able to carry the new double burden of elder-caregiving and full-time career. Many will have to switch to part-time jobs, forfeit promotions, or quit their jobs altogether, unless they demand reforms in public policy and decent eldercare. The cruel choice for a growing number of menopausal-aged women will be: Do I take care of my mother in her old age, or provide for independence in my own old age?

No wonder, just beneath the calm, composed surface of many middle-aged women, one finds bag-lady fears.

Across Color, Class, and Culture Lines

~

$\mathscr{T}$he chief reason for the silence and apprehension surrounding the subject of menopause in American society is our phobia about aging. Cross-cultural studies of women and menopause reveal that the Change of Life is experienced differently depending on one's cultural assumptions about aging, femininity, and the societal role of the older woman. When the American sociologist Pauline Bart studied anthropological accounts of the status of women in a large number of cultures, she found that the feminine role assumed by a woman in her fertile years was in all cultures reversed after menopause.

Anthropologist Mary Catherine Bateson points out: "In many societies women are granted a greater degree of freedom after menopause than they were permitted in their reproductive years. This may be because women no longer represent a risk of 'pollution,' or no longer need to be sequestered as sex objects through whom their husbands might be dishonored." Indian women of the Rajput caste do not complain of depression or psychological symptoms of menopause since they are freed from veiled invisibility and at last are able to sit and joke with the men, reports anthropologist Marcha Flint. Furthermore, in some traditional societies such as Iran's women only come into their own when they have an adult son. Bateson describes how grown-up sons literally pay court to their mothers, visiting them with news and flowers.

Women in Asian countries report fewer and less severe symptoms than menopausal women in the West—even though the mean age at menopause is the same across the board (slightly over fifty-one years). These findings were presented at the Sixth International Congress on the Menopause, held in Bangkok in late 1990. The study included women from Hong Kong, Malaysia, the Philippines, South Korea, Taiwan, Indonesia, and Singapore.

In China, where age is venerated, menopausal symptoms are rarely reported. Similarly, anthropologist Margaret Lock observed after studying a thousand Japanese women that 65 percent of them consider menopause uneventful. The Japanese language does not even have a word for hot flashes. (A report in *The Lancet*, however, describes "sinking spells" among Japanese women, rather like the swooning of Victorian women.) However, the virtual nonexistence of hot flashes in Japanese women is *not cultural*, according to Lock. It is due primarily to their different diet and the vigorous physical exercise built into the life of even elderly Japanese women. The fish-dominated diet of Japanese women yields high levels of soy (a source of estrogen) and calcium. And because most Japanese women have small kitchens, they walk or bike daily to the shops and hand-carry groceries back home, routinely enjoying a much higher degree of exercise than most middle-class women undertake in the West. As a result, menopausal women in Japan are not as prone to menopausal health problems as Western women are; they have a much lower incidence of heart disease, osteoporosis, and breast cancer. Although only two percent of them take hormones, Japanese women in general are the longest-living women in the world.

In America, youth and desirability go hand in hand, and the role for the older woman is uncertain at best. Ours is also an overweight, underexercised culture, particularly in the upper age brackets. Very few roles or jobs in the information age demand that American women over forty exert much more physical effort than opening their car doors and microwaves. But although menopause in the U. S. is defined primarily in hormonal terms, cultural attitudes do cut deeply, casting the signs and symptoms in a negative light. Of 2,500 Massachusetts women aged forty-five to fifty-five studied by Harvard sociologist John McKinlay and epidemiologist Sonja McKinlay, most anticipated menopause with relief. But for those whose self-worth rests primarily in appearance and sexual desirability, passing fifty is like *taking the veil*; suddenly they feel invisible.

Although I did not undertake a "scientific" sampling of American women's menopausal experiences, I did interview more than one hundred women from diverse racial, class, and educational backgrounds. I discovered that the women who enjoy a boost in postmenopausal status and self-esteem are those who perform roles in which intellect, judgment, creativity, or spiritual strength is primarily valued—politicians, educators, lawmakers, doctors, nurse-supervisors, therapists, writers, artists, clergywomen, etc.—while women whose worth was earlier judged primarily on their looks and sex appeal—movie actresses, performers, many full-time wives and mothers—are diminished in status. We know that middle-class housewives who are overinvolved with their children are the most likely to suffer depression in this stage of life. But they, too, are able to change stale self-images if they are willing to leave the comfort of familiarity and take the risk of starting a new direction in their Second Adulthood. Women who build close bonds to grandchildren may make themselves indispensable and often enjoy a tender and playful intimacy that brings them closer than they were to their own children.

African-American women in general are more likely than white women to pass through menopause with no psychological problems. Why? I wondered. After this book was first published, a friend and former professor of adult development, Clementine Pugh, gathered together a fascinating discussion group with twenty accomplished African-American women, most of them educators with advanced degrees. They agreed that African-American women do not measure their femininity and sensuality only by how they look. Nor is their self-worth attached to their age—how young they look. A great deal of a black woman's sexuality is defined by her spiritual strength, a strength dictated by her historical situation.

Middle-class African-American women come out of matrilineal tradition. Never having been pampered by life or put on a pedestal while they were young, as white women are, they gain in prestige and self-esteem as they enter middle age. And they definitely do not give up on themselves as sexually desirable or desirous. What's more, sensuality, for the African-American woman, is not related to the European-American anorexic body type. Stop and think about the many great older black women entertainers who sing and shake and bring the house down— from Moms Mabley and Ma Rainey to Della Reese, Patti Labelle, and even the opera superstar Jessye Norman. The older and broader they are, it seems, the more shamelessly lusty they can be. In short, menopause is more readily accepted as an integral part of life.

Women of color, however, do have their own physical vulnerability—fibroid tumors—a vulnerability often worsened by cultural attitudes. Fibroids are benign growths found in 20 percent of all women. They are far more common among African-American women than among white women, according to the National Black Women's

Health Project. They often lead women to unnecessary hysterectomies. As a result, says Frances Dorey, chair of the project, "Black women are lucky if they even make it to menopause with a uterus." The medical reason they have a higher incidence of fibroids remains unknown (African-American women are generally excluded from the studies or are unidentified by race in clinical trials).

Pamela Pilate's job as a nurse with the giant California HMO Kaiser Permanente is to do menopause education. Many state employees and low-income women come to her classes in downtown Los Angeles. She holds two kinds of classes, and when I asked her if she had noticed any cultural differences in attitudes women bring in, Pilate said something startling even to herself:

"The white women attend my menopause class. The black and Hispanic women come to my hysterectomy class." Women of color or low income who present an assigned Medicaid doctor with symptoms common to the "fearsome forties"—heavy, clotted bleeding and cramps such as they haven't had since before bearing their children—are most likely to be steered toward a hysterectomy. By the time they are referred to a nurse-counselor like Pamela Pilate, they already have a date for surgery.

As an African-American woman herself, Pilate is dismayed by how passively many of her patients approach this surrender of their reproductive organs. "When women of color have female problems, their usual reaction is to wait," the nurse-practitioner reports. "It's denial or fear." Lack of basic medical knowledge about their own bodies also plays a large part. As Pilate notes, "White women look for other alternatives—nutrition, herbs, or less invasive surgical procedures for removing the benign growths." By the time the black women come to her hysterectomy class, they have waited a long time to see a doctor, and they are either in pain or suffering from heavy bleeding or urinary problems. The fibroid may have grown to the size of a grapefruit.

When Pilate inquires if their surgeon also plans to remove their ovaries, most of the women have no idea. "Usually, they don't know the function of their ovaries."

Pilate's lecture stresses that hysterectomy is a last resort. She also emphasizes that as a woman approaches menopause, uterine fibroids usually shrink if she doesn't take HRT. "But the women I see have a cut-and-dried attitude. 'This is part of life, what else? Let's get it over with.'" The highest point of consciousness-raising Pilate can usually orchestrate is to get the women to go back and ask, "Okay, doctor, why do you think that my ovaries should go?"

In *Essence* magazine Dr. Ezra C. Davidson, Jr., president of the American College of Obstetricians and Gynecologists, confirmed Pilate's anecdotal observation: "By the time black women get into a doctor's office, their presentation of fibroid tumors is often dramatic."

"You're going to have a hysterectomy, just like my sister, cousin, mother, aunt, daughter, etc.," was the message repeated like a folk belief to Marsha Carruthers of Grand Rapids, Michigan, when she consulted friends and physicians about her fibroids. A professional health consultant to women of color all over the country, Carruthers was adamant about avoiding this surgery. She read about barks and herbs said to be effective in reducing menstrual flow and benign tumors—white oak bark, slippery elm bark, witch hazel, etc. She took the herbs in capsules and altered her diet radically, cutting out red meat, sugar, white flour, and processed foods. Within a month her cycle regulated itself.

Cross-cultural research in the United Kingdom brought to the surface some striking differences between American and European attitudes. While race is a profound determinant of how a woman experiences menopause in the United States, class seems to be the paramount factor influencing a British woman's self-image as well as her access to health care. European women, on the whole, are better informed than American women about hormone replacement therapy. The media in Britain and Europe have given considerable attention to the pros and cons of hormones over the past five years. But outside of that narrow consideration, I found, many women put blinders on and refuse to acknowledge the deeper psychosexual questions and long-term health questions raised by this transition.

"My response to the word menopause is so overlaid with doom, which it shouldn't be," mused Fay Weldon, the British novelist famed for her witty sendups of male sexual vanity. "It's a word used by men to define the cause of your being, as they see it, horrible, miserable, and unattractive. If women embrace this as a term, they're inviting a definition which is diminishing to them. Hormone levels are not the total sum of a human being: There is more to their misery than that."

In her words I heard a common discomfort about committing oneself to the existence of such a problematic passage. The popular novelist Barbara Taylor Bradford put up an even more defiant resistance. Remembering as a girl how her aunts in England had talked about the Change in hushed, somewhat ominous tones, she simply vowed to herself when she hit fifty, "To hell with that. I'm not going to pay any attention. It's not going to have any effect on me!"

This attitude might be characterized as meaning: *If I don't acknowledge it, it doesn't exist.* The same attitude was put slightly differently by Eve Pollard, the normally outspoken British newspaper editor of the *Sunday Express:* "If you don't talk about it, you might just float through it." She acknowledges, however, "We certainly share the American nervousness about getting older."

At the opposite end of the spectrum from those who do their best to deny aging and ignore menopause are those who proclaim themselves better than ever—and usually sing the praises of hormone replacement. Kate O'Mara, a popular British actress, was in Hollywood, on camera in a bubble bath, playing Joan Collins's younger sister in an episode of *Dynasty* when the biological clock suddenly clanged. She was forty-six or -seven. *Dear God, this bath is hot,* she thought. More cold water, please! But it wasn't the water. It was, inescapably, drenchingly, and most unsexily, a hot flash. O'Mara leapt from the bath and thought, *That's it. It's all over.*

Since that incident ten years ago, the volatile actress has discovered hormone replacement therapy and become a total devotee. Her publicity photos present a bust-thrusting sex siren propped on stiletto heels with a plume of streaked brown hair, a performer who obviously takes considerable care in the attempt to freeze time. Feminists attack her for doing all this only to look attractive to men. O'Mara, divorced for the last twenty years, denies the charge:

"What they don't understand is the longer my looks and my energy last, the longer my career lasts. It doesn't matter whether you ever want to see a man in your bed again." O'Mara proselytizes to younger actresses. "When you're my age, you must go on HRT. It is wonderful, it's brilliant, it's the last great frontier to women's true emancipation." The actress doesn't mind at all disclosing her age: fifty-six. As she told me, that's the whole point.

I found a whole arc of subtle distinctions in between these two perspectives. Dorothy Rowe, a sage British sociologist in her sixties who writes and gardens in Sheffield, represents the sensible-shoes outlook. "In Britain, there simply isn't this feeling that you have to stay young. Cher and Joan Collins are not role models here. The Queen is a role model. A lot of women dress like her. Sensible, not flashy."

Eve Pollard expressed the different perspective of a younger, more combative generation: "Sharing the Queen's attitude is fine and good *only* if you're upper class. If you are just out there watching Woody Allen going for twenty-one-year-olds, you know which way this thing goes."

The extreme version of the natural menopause view is represented by Germaine Greer's brilliant polemic *The Change*. She counsels women to resort to behaving like crones as the way to register their visibility. "You're expected to be dreadful. So you might as well act it." Making a talisman of her own frustrating experience with hormone replacement therapy, Greer faults the medical establishment for conspiring to make women dependent on pills and patches that have been woefully undertested. But her bitter manifesto serves also to blind women to the renewal of energy, new passions and purposes possible at this time of life.

To most Europeans, expectations of life beyond age fifty are still based on outdated stereotypes of an older genoration. The retirement age for women in Britain is still sixty. Many approach retirement with the attitude, "I've had a long, hard life, and retirement is the rest I deserve." They seem to accept, along with Germaine Greer, that "the climacteric is the antechamber of death."

In fact, death for the average fifty-year-old British woman is more than thirty years away. Who wants to rest for thirty years? Even if you want to, that much rest is hazardous to your health.

By contrast, a woman who has provided for her health and salted away her own employment pension, and who believes, at sixty, that she *deserves* a full and interesting life, will probably have cultivated many different skills and great and small passions. She very likely has goals and dreams that will outlast her life span, intentionally so. It is women like her who will probably seek out hormone replacement and who, with their renewed vitality and self-confidence, burst out of old constraints.

"It's all part of having more money in their pockets, the kids having gone, the mortgage being close to paid off," as British MP Edwina Currie describes the new prototype of her middle-aged female constituents. "They've gone for better promotions, they're working full-time, and they know the boss needs them. Ten years ago they would sit quietly during a political meeting and look at their nails. Now they ask the fiercest questions I get. It's a total sea change of attitude amongst women of our age group."

Another reason for the fear inspired by the prospect of menopause is the assumption that it takes place at a single point in time. Women are very frightened that at age forty-nine, all these things they've read about—heart disease, osteoporosis, vaginal atrophy—will happen at once. No distinction is made between women's lives at fifty and at seventy. We would never do this with men.

It is important, then, to distinguish among the various phases of the long menopausal passage. Archie Bunker probably spoke for many impatient husbands when he pressed his long-suffering wife in an 1972 episode of *All in the Family*.

ARCHIE: Edith, if you're gonna have a change of life, you gotta do it right now. I'm gonna give you just thirty seconds. Now come on, CHANGE!

EDITH: Can I finish my soup first?

More changes probably take place during this passage than at any other time in a woman's adult life. It is fortunate, then, that this passage takes some years to complete. As one moves through the physical, psychological, social, and spiritual aspects of the transition, dramatic shifts in perspective occur. There may be a transformation in the sense of time, of self in relation to others, and a rethinking of the negative vs. positive aspects of moving into a new and unfamiliar state of being.

The acute period of biological passage, or ovarian transition, spans five to seven years—usually forty-seven or forty-eight to the mid-fifties. But it is the beginning of a long and little-mapped stage of postreproductive life. I propose three demarcations of this Second Adulthood for contemporary Western women: *perimenopause* (start of the transition); *menopause* (completion of the ovarian transition); and a stage I will call *coalescence*—the mirror image of adolescence—in which women can tap into the new vitality Margaret Mead called "postmenopausal zest."

The
Perimenopause
Panic

$\mathcal{T}$he vast majority of women have no idea they are in something called "perimenopause." Yet a woman's attitude and awareness going into this first phase of the silent passage have a profound impact on how it is experienced. The spectrum of signs and symptoms in perimenopause is bafflingly broad. One woman will brush it off—"I feel hot for a few seconds a couple of times a day, but not enough to bother me"—while another is terrified that she will flare purple and start leaking drops of perspiration during another business conference or forget phone numbers she just looked up. A third woman, who complains of waking up four or five times a night, swamped in sweat, changing nightgowns, having Thermostat Wars with her husband, is mistakenly diagnosed as being in clinical depression. In truth, she is suffering from the effects of serious sleep deprivation.

It hardly seems possible that these people are all talking about the same organic process.

Entering perimenopause is very much like entering puberty. It is reminiscent of the first time one got one's period—the I-could-die feeling when a girlfriend whispered, "You have a spot on the back of your skirt," and you had to back out of the glee club rehearsal so no one would see. And now, at the dignified apex of one's adulthood, to have to worry about being hit with surprise periods or hot flashes, night sweats and insomnia, sudden bouts of waistline bloat, possibly heart palpitations, crying for no reason or temper outbursts, maybe migraines, incontinence, itchy, crawly skin, memory lapses—my God, what's going on?

It is during perimenopause—in their forties—that women feel most estranged from their bodies. Half of all women who have hot flashes will begin feeling them while they are still menstruating normally, starting as early as age forty. Studies show that most women have hot flashes for two years. One quarter of women have them for five years. And 10 percent have them for the rest of their lives.

The first sign of perimenopause is very often not hot flashes but gushing: a sudden heavy flow of blood that may be dark or clotted and that may seep through the normal protection. Dr. Allen tells patients in their forties, "Your cycle will get longer or shorter, lighter or heavier, closer together or farther apart. This is all normal." She adds, "Almost everybody bleeds erratically during perimenopause."

(It happens when we stop ovulating every month. The months when ovulation doesn't occur, we produce no progesterone—the hormone ordinarily responsible for flushing the lining of the uterus. The endometrial lining becomes thicker and may not be entirely discarded until the next cycle, when the body deals with the previous buildup.)

One month a woman may have a heavy period, another month nothing; all of a sudden she may develop cysts in her breast, or functional ovarian cysts, and two months or a year later she may be back to normal. The reason for all the volatility is that hormone levels are surging and falling in frantic response to desperate signals from the brain to the pituitary. Her menstrual cycle not only becomes erratic but is uncoupled from her temperature and sleep cycles and affects her appetite, sexual interest, and overall sense of well-being. The body's whole balance is thrown off.

When does it happen? For Barbara Bush it was fifty. Contemporary women should expect it much earlier. The latest surveys reveal a surprising number of women in their early forties are perimenopausal. Researchers admit they have underestimated the number of younger women who experience all the symptoms of menopause even though they still have periods.

Phyllis Mansfield, an academic researcher at Pennsylvania State University who studies female cycles, registered the first signs of the Change in herself in her early forties. Having always had a normal and very predictable cycle, she was unnerved when her periods became heavier and more frequent. "I would have to schedule family camping trips and conferences around my cycle." Although she studied and went for checkups, still, in the back of her mind, was a common fear: *Are my organs deteriorating?*

She noticed something odd, too, about her moods. As a researcher she knew that premenstrual stress occurs after ovulation. But when one's cycle becomes erratic, with periods every two or three weeks, or two or three months apart, how does one know when, or if, ovulation occurs?

"I'd have a really long period of magnificent energy and acute mental functioning, even brilliance, when I'm never tired, always very up, producing like crazy. At first I thought, *Oh! so this is going to be part of my new personality.* Then just as suddenly I fell into a period of intense anxiety—and that lasted for a month. I thought, *So, is this it?* But once I got my period, the despond just lifted and dissipated in one day. So then you think, *What happens when there are no more cycles? Is there one mood that persists? Is it permanent mellowing? Permanent anything?"*

While this can be very unsettling, the important thing to know is that perimenopause is *a temporary phenomenon.* It is a time to plan to reduce stressful pressures wherever possible and to pamper yourself a little bit. There is no reason to panic or drive yourself into a frenzy looking for the perfect "cure." Resistance to accepting that one has entered the long passage leading out of youth and fertility and into unfamiliar territory is perfectly understandable. But remaining resistant to that reality blocks a woman from entering her Second Adulthood.

As a practitioner in New York City, Dr. Patricia Allen has observed over the past three years that the silence about menopause has turned into an obsession. "Baby boom women come into my office now in an information-feeding frenzy," she says. "They want the perfect treatment without consequences." She tells women, "It is important that you make informed choices. But you also have to recognize that everything we do, or don't do, has some price."

Silent Changes

$\mathcal{T}$he acceleration of bone loss begins during the peri-menopausal phase, as do other changes in the long-term health status of the older woman. "The problem is, nobody *feels* the bone they're losing until it's too late," says Dr. Lindsay. "That is, osteoporosis is without symptoms until it becomes disease."

We build all the bone we are going to make by the time we're thirty-five. "Women really start to lose bone mass at forty," says Richard Bockman, head of the endocrine department and codirector of the Osteoporosis Center at the Hospital for Special Surgery in Manhattan. "Bone loss occurs rapidly even before the menopause, then accelerates during the menopause as hormones fall off, and eventually tapers off to a slower rate of loss about ten years after the onset of menopause." Generally, this timetable of bone loss occurs in all white women, according to the National Osteoporosis Foundation in Washington, D.C., though not necessarily for women of color.

Similarly, silent changes in the blood vessels that nourish the heart begin taking place during perimenopause. Estrogen makes a woman's blood vessels more elastic. Nature provides this relaxing hormone in abundance during the reproductive years because whenever a woman is pregnant, her blood volume expands. If her blood vessels were as rigid as a man's, the increase in blood pressure would kill both mother and fetus in about the fifth month, according to Dr. Estelle Ramey, professor emeritus and physiologist at Georgetown University.

"So all during your young years, whether you get pregnant or not, you walk around with more elastic blood vessels—until menopause," says Dr. Ramey. When a woman stops producing estrogen, her good cholesterol (HDL) level falls. Bad (LDL) cholesterol levels start increasing during the transition *into* menopause, as confirmed by the National Institutes of Health. Thus begins for women the narrowing of arteries that will gradually expose them to the cardiovascular disease from which estrogen protected them during their fertile years.

In addition to noticing a lessening of lubrication in the vagina, many women notice bladder problems or suffer the embarrassment of feeling a sudden urge to urinate before they can make it to the bathroom. This "urge incontinence" is common, though little discussed, and may be associated with lack of estrogen. Also, the uterus changes shape as women get older and may come to press on the organs of the urinary tract. Male urologists usually shun female patients with such chronic complaints. There may be no more than fifty female urologists in the United States. One of them, Dr. Suzanne Frye in Manhattan, says the problem is easily correctable in most cases. A drug called Ditropan can reverse this bladder instability and change a menopausal woman's life.

"But I have cystic breasts, so I can't take hormones, right?" women would often ask in the group interviews. Cystic breasts are not uncommon at this stage. Dr. Hiram Cody, one of the top breast surgeons at New York Hospital, explains, "During the perimenopausal period breasts can become lumpier and more tender than before, due to surges of excess estrogen. It subsides within a year after periods stop."

Should women who are suffering the worst symptoms of menopause and accelerated health deficits be able to start hormone replacement therapy during perimenopause? The old dogma said no. Dr. Allen summarizes current practice.

"We know now that there are good medical reasons for some women to begin hormone replacement therapy during the perimenopause years. Acceleration of bone loss begins, risks for coronary artery disease start to increase, atrophy of breast and genital tissue starts. And so, most doctors now believe that a woman who is bothered by menopausal symptoms, if she chooses HRT, should be treated before the cessation of her periods."

According to Howard Zacur, M.D., Ph.D., director of the Johns Hopkins Estrogen Consultation Service, recognizing perimenopause as a distinct stage before actual menopause is essential in order to provide the correct medical treatment. The type of hormone replacement therapy given to women in true menopause is not sufficient to halt perimenopausal symptoms, he says. During perimenopause the body may manufacture its own estrogen now and then, causing an excess of the hormone. "The way around it is to give a dose of estrogen high enough to suppress the body from making its own, such as that contained in oral contraceptive pills."

Low-dose oral contraceptives deal with the continuing risk of pregnancy even as they alleviate hot flashes and irregular or heavy bleeding.

Dancing Around Depression

~

"*I* think I'm going crazy" is a frightened admission Dr. Morris Notelovitz frequently hears at the Women's Health Center in Gainesville, Florida, where he sees extreme cases. "Many women feel it's very difficult to concentrate. They can hear what's going on, they know they're there, but it's as though their body is just witnessing." These are the women whose hormones are falling and spiking and falling again, six times a day or even a half dozen times within an hour. They feel—and, in fact, they are—out of control of their bodies. They may also feel at the mercy of erratic moods. Is it all in their minds?

Whether or not depression is associated with menopause has been a subject of intense debate, mostly because of a looseness of terminology and the Freudian hangover. Freud related the loss of reproductive potential with mourning and melancholia. Indeed, it was common in our mothers' day for middle- and upper-middle class women in the Change to be institutionalized. "Nervous breakdown" it was called, because nobody associated their intense if temporary depression with the temporary breakdown of hormonal balance.

The mood swings so characteristic of perimenopause may bring on sadness, malaise, mild depression, irritability, poor concentration—in general, the feeling of being on a roller coaster. Western medicine still fosters the erroneous assumption that these *temporary* mental symptoms herald a marked deterioration in the mental health of postmenopausal women. Exactly the opposite is true. It is women in their mid- to late forties who manifest a peak in minor mental symptoms in the five years *immediately prior* to the end of their cycles. Something changes profoundly between the years of entry to this passage and the completion of it, when the hallmark is a euphoric burst of new energy. Studies now confirm that women in the postmenopausal years show *less* evidence of any psychological problems than younger women.

Yet outmoded cultural attitudes swing tremendous weight in influencing how a woman copes at this time of life. Seeking to correct this oversight, Dr. C. B. Ballinger, an eminent Scottish psychiatrist, academic researcher, and consultant at Royal Dundee Liff Hospital, found in a review of recent British and Dutch population surveys that "complaints of 'mental imbalance,' fatigue, depression, and irritability were most common in women who were still menstruating and reached a peak . . . in women reporting irregular menstrual periods who could be considered immediately pre-menopausal." Ballinger's own study confirmed that it was the women aged forty-five to forty-nine years *and still menstruating* who had the highest levels of negative mental effects. But she then followed up and found from population surveys that "women in the postmenopausal years show less evidence of psychiatric disturbance than younger women." Her conclusions are consistent with those reached by several other researchers using very different survey techniques.

The much-publicized Massachusetts Women's Health Study reported in a 1986 Harvard Medical School publication that "depression in middle-aged women is associated mainly with events and circumstances unrelated to the hormonal changes that occur at menopause." Epidemiologist Sonja McKinlay, coauthor of the study with her husband, John, insisted in an interview: "Most women just go straight through menopause, no problem, none, nor with irritability."

Try out that line on a room full of menopausal-aged women and one is guaranteed a laugh. The McKinlays' conclusion—that depression at this stage is associated *only* with external "social circumstances"—was suspect since it was a paper-and-pencil questionnaire and no measurements had been taken of the actual hormone levels in peri- and postmenopausal women.

Of the many stories I had been told by women themselves, a typical description of menopausal malaise came from a woman I'll call Nora. A former tavern owner, she was remarried as she started her forties and had happily moved to the country. She had never been depressed before. At forty-six, when she began skipping periods, a fog of indeterminate sadness came over her from out of left field.

"I'd go out and walk for five miles every morning on a country road, sun shining, birds singing—and tears would start running down my cheeks. Why? I kept looking at my life—Was there anything to validate this depression?" she recalled asking. "Nothing. I was normally very up. My doctor told me I was too young for menopause. Then I remembered times in adolescence when I'd come home from school, go into my room, sit down on my bed, and cry. That's when I knew. Whatever these doctors say, it's my hormones." Her malaise, although frightening at the time, lifted within several months.

It is true that *clinical* depression subsides in women over fifty, and irritability and depression in middle-aged women do have many other sources. But mood changes are so commonly mentioned by women in the perimenopause phase, why should women be told there is no hormonal basis for feeling depressed?

"That's looking at major depression as a disease," stresses Dr. Howard Fillit, a gerontologist at Mount Sinai Hospital in New York City. "A woman comes into a doctor's office at age fifty-one with the menopause and says, 'Doctor, I can't function very well in the office. I think I have memory loss, I can't pay attention to my work, and I feel really depressed.' If the doctor reads the literature, he knows that there's no major association of depression with the menopause, so he says, 'C'mon, you're crazy.' If the doctor was aware that these complaints and symptoms are real, although they may not qualify as a disease, this problem could be dealt with in a constructive manner." Up to 80 percent of menopausal women in self-report studies describe feeling nervousness and irritability.

In fact, estrogen does improve mood and the sense of psychological well-being even in well-adjusted women who have no distressing menopausal symptoms, according to a study done by Dr. Edward Ditkoff at the University of Southern California School of Medicine. Women in the random study who were given the standard dose of 0.625 mg of estrogen a day showed a decided improvement in depression scores and were more optimistic and confident than those given placebos. Neurobiologically estrogen has chemical effects on the brain that are similar to those of antidepressants. The most experienced researchers say that when estrogen levels in the blood are very low, a woman might start to feel a bit sad or blue or notice irritability or mood swings, but not of a clinical magnitude.

That is the key distinction: Women low in estrogen often have feelings of malaise, as opposed to suffering from the DSM-III criteria for depression as disease (the criteria used in the McKinlays' Massachusetts study). Unless there are also underlying causes, the blues that may color the years leading up to menopause are a temporary phenomenon.

Two areas of behavior have been found by Dr. Ballinger to be very widely influenced by menopause: Sleep and sexual response. Indeed, one of the most common sources of mood changes at this stage of life is broken sleep. Night sweats that awaken a woman several times, interrupting REM sleep night after night, can easily produce all the consequences of sleep deprivation. A major function of REM sleep is to allow important brain cells to rest and replenish their chemical stores, according to the latest dream research at Harvard Medical School. It also releases sleep-promoting transmitters and is crucial in regulating body temperature. So it should come as no surprise that a person awakened by temperature aberrations, and deprived of the REM sleep needed to reset the body's thermostat, is stuck in a vicious circle.

"These are real symptoms. Don't think you're crazy," Dr. Robert Lindsay tells his patients. A good-humored Scottish-born endocrinologist, Lindsay was asked by New York State to set up a bone center in conjunction with Columbia University. His clinic at the Helen Hayes Bone Center is now booked almost a year in advance because, he says, women are not getting reasonable answers to their questions about menopause elsewhere. "The reason estrogen works so well in curing menopausal depression is that it restores REM sleep," he says. "Once women can sleep better, they're fine. They don't need a psychiatrist or a divorce."

To be sure, when Sonja McKinlay went back to do a five-year follow-up of the 2,570 middle-aged women in the Massachusetts study, she had to backtrack somewhat. Women who experienced a long perimenopausal period— more than a two-year transition—had a "moderately increased, but transitory, risk of depression," reports the 1992 paper. And this depression was prompted not by unfortunate social circumstances; it was due to menopausal symptoms. There is a parallel here between puberty and perimenopause. In both instances the effects on mood can be sharp but short-lived, as the body adjusts to a new hormonal milieu.

Women I have interviewed often describe a "pit" or "low" during their mid- to late forties, complicated in many cases by the confusing symptoms of perimenopause. In the course of research for my latest book, *New Passages: Mapping Your Life Across Time*, I did national surveys of over seven thousand women. Those with the poorest sense of well-being were, on average, forty-seven years old—the pits. But it comes back strong in the early fifties. Those enjoying the highest sense of well-being were fifty-three—the peak.

Facing the entryway of any new major passage in the life cycle is always far more daunting than actually moving through the transition. So many women in postmenopause have described to me, sometimes with bemused amazement, how vital and energetic and *focused* they feel. I was amused myself when I had a late lunch recently with a male friend in his mid-fifties. After walking thirty city blocks to the restaurant, I found my companion already halfway through his soup. "I just couldn't wait," he said. "You're still going strong and you probably got up at six o'clock this morning."

I was taken aback. "How did you know?"

"Because women your age always seem to get up at six in the morning. You're more energetic than ever—just at the time we men are starting to wind down." He was right about that switch, generally speaking, but such a comforting perspective is not real or believable for women until they themselves have actually come through the Change.

The passage of menopause is inextricably bound up with other common life events and cultural determinants. Harsh losses such as a parent's life-threatening illness or death are new and real around this time. The inescapable evidence of physical aging and the cruel penalties of ageism also register. Women are brutally premature in disqualifying *themselves* as no longer attractive to men, simply because they are no longer young. And there is the artifact of generation. Few women in middle age today were prepared, professionally or emotionally, for the reality that being an earner becomes central to the self-esteem—and often the survival —of women in the middle years. The shift in body chemistry may be a casual matter compared with the faltering of one's former identity, as the role of mother becomes distant and custodial if not outright rejected. The menopausal identity crisis is exaggerated if at the same time one begins to lose social contact through divorce, retirement, or widowhood.

Disengagement from the mothering role and the end of fertility, however, turn out to be precursors to the beneficent change in body chemistry and mental outlook summed up in the term "postmenopausal zest."

So, despite the danger zone through which most women will pass in their late forties, a mobilization usually begins shortly after menopause, and a profound change in self-concept begins to register with rising exhilaration for many women as they move into their fifties. They often break the seal on repressed angers. They overcome the habits of trying to be perfect and of needing to make everyone love them. They may shed the terror of living without a man that trapped them in a dead or destructive marriage. Many women, during the decade of the mid-forties to the mid-fifties, find the sustained courage to extricate themselves from lives of desperate repetition.

The sense of well-being is more than happiness, the latter generally conveying relief from pent-up frustration or deprivation. Well-being registers deep in our unconscious, as a sustained background tone of equanimity—a calm, composed sense of all-rightness—that remains behind the more intense contrasts of daily events, including periods of unhappiness. I studied the phenomenon for an earlier book, *Pathfinders*, sending out extensive Life History question-

naires to women and men all over the United States. On the
life cycle graphs plotted from the results of the 60,000
returned questionnaires, that sense of well-being gradually
rises for women through the mid-fifties, reaching a high
point around fifty-seven, when it takes off and soars. The
issue of trying too hard to please is, for most, surmounted.
Women begin at last to value *themselves*.

Several caveats must be added to these generalized statements on depression and menopause. Depression is correlated with surgical menopause. Most women feel relieved
immediately after a hysterectomy. But a review of research
by psychologist Ellen McGrath, editor of the American
Psychological Association's 1990 task force report *Women
and Depression*, shows that women who have had hysterectomies are twice as likely to become depressed over time.
The impact on sexual responsiveness and desire may be a
major culprit. It is also likely that a woman who has suffered
from phases of depression in the past will react in the same
way during the transition of menopause.

The Massachusetts study confirms these observations.
The two groups of women found most likely to become
depressed are those who have experienced depression prior
to menopause and women who have had hysterectomies.
"Depression is associated with surgical menopause, but it
may be the cause rather than the consequence of the
surgery since the group of women who undergo hysterectomies is atypical," reports the study. Among those who were
found on follow-up to have had the highest rates of depression, usually during perimenopause (apart from those with
hysterectomies), were widowed, divorced, and separated
women with less than twelve years of education. Never-
married women showed the lowest rates of depression.
Married women fell between the two extremes.

Women who are used to having mood swings with PMS
appear to be very sensitive to hormonal fluctuation, Dr.

Allen has observed in her practice. "These women may be at risk for depression in the perimenopausal period, when hormonal fluctuations are unpredictable and most violent." Again there is good news: Such women experience great relief when they reach the postmenopausal period. They are released from the treacherous mood baths of their reproductive years and feel a consistency of calmness at last.

"Stress Menopause"

〜

$\mathcal{I}$t used to be that a reliable guide to when you might expect menopause is when your mother experienced it. But the mothers of today's groundbreaking women knew nothing like the level of workplace stress and environmental toxins we live with today. Acute or prolonged stress has been shown to increase the severity of symptoms in phase one of menopause and may even precipitate it prematurely. In fact, severe stress can reduce ovarian function and precipitate a temporary menopause at any time from the late thirties on. It may happen around the time of death of a close relative or other traumatic events. The phenomenon is similar to that experienced by a college student who is up against exams and who misses a period.

An anesthesiologist who deals with life and death every day, running an intensive care unit in a midwestern hospital, had her own life turned upside down in her fortieth year.

"I had a fire in my home that was rather devastating," she recounts. Having outstripped her own expectations, she was habituated to a high-performance life. "Of course, I said, oh, well, it was just a fire. I lived in a hotel for six months with two children to care for and continued working very hard—there was my team to run at the hospital—and I was determined that the fire would not have any impact on my life. It was just 'pedal to the metal' and go right on."

Noticing she was a little frantic, the anesthesiologist began vigorously exercising an hour or two daily, in addition to her work and parenting responsibilities. She dropped down to a scrawny 105 pounds and couldn't sleep. "I was anxious and depressed, though I didn't acknowledge it. Suddenly my periods, which have never been that regular, weren't around at all. And when I did sleep, I was waking up five or six times a night and throwing the covers off." Her dentist husband said to her after a few weeks, "Well, honey, I think you're in menopause."

"What! I am only forty years old, of course I am not in menopause." But the very next day she did her blood test. "My FSH and LH were off the wall and my estrogen was very low," she was chagrined to discover. "It took me about five minutes to put an Estraderm patch on my behind [a means of delivering estrogen through the skin], and within three days I felt my old self again," continued the anesthesiologist. After a couple of months she stopped the exogenous estrogen, and her hormone levels remained normal. "It seems I had a case of temporary menopause, due to much stress," the physician diagnosed herself after the fact. It might also have been precipitated by the extreme weight loss, as found in young marathon runners with no body fat. "In any case," she says, "I look upon that little visit of menopause as one of the greatest gifts that God has ever given me because it made me quite sympathetic to older women."

Everyone wants to be the person she was before. But your body is signaling that this is truly a Change of Life: You cannot put the same demands on it and expect it to be there for you whenever you have a period of high demand or unexpected stress. You cannot continue indefinitely being the same person as your younger self. To attempt to be is the best way to precipitate depression.

Chemotherapy can also bring on a premature menopause. A head nurse at a major metropolitan hospital told me her personal story, which, sadly, is no longer unusual. "I was diagnosed with breast cancer when I was thirty-seven and I had a mastectomy and a year of chemotherapy. It was the chemotherapy—the drug Cytoxan—that caused ovarian failure."

The most unsettling aspect of this crisis period in the nurse's life was caused by her own—and her doctors'—ignorance about the impact of premature menopause. Known for her natural organizational skills and unflappable temperament, she had organized patient care in a high-demand environment for fifteen years. The untimely menopause caused her months of interrupted sleep and insomnia, along with mounting anxiety and feelings of depression.

"Suddenly, without any change of environment, my organization skills were compromised," noticed the nurse. "I was much slower. It was very troublesome." As soon as the reason became clear, medication corrected the problems. Some women are lucky, however. Once the chemotherapy is over, they do resume cycling naturally. But not all doctors are aware of these complications.

Menopause Moms

Women having babies in their forties know they have departed from life cycle norms when they have to put on reading glasses to breast-feed. "I can't get him on the nipple without them!" squeals Jane, a former Sixties radical turned doting first-time mother at forty-two.

"I am the only self-avowed menopausal mother in my son's preschool," was the amusing confession of Marcia Wallace, an actress who has worked on *The Bob Newhart Show* and *The Simpsons*. Marcia has cultivated the zany image of her celebrity with a red corkscrew-curled mop and loud colors and chandelier-size earrings. But what struck me were the consequences of reversed life stages that her story represents. A late bloomer, Marcia devoted her young years to pursuing her career and postponed the personal commitments usually made by a woman in her twenties until she reached her forties. She married for the first time at forty-three.

"I figured, by then, all I had left was one egg on a walker," Marcia quips. So she became an adoptive mother two years later. And a mere year after that—guess what? Marcia's new variant on women's life stages might be called The Compressed Life: marriage at forty-three, motherhood at forty-five, and menopause at forty-six.

A late first pregnancy often triggers an earlier menopause. A hotshot businesswoman who delivered her first child in her mid-forties found herself afterward often drenched in sweat and gloomy. She told herself it must be postpartum depression (which is, indeed, rooted in the temporary depletion of estrogen following childbirth.) When the symptoms went on for two years, she began to wonder. But the last thing she would have done was to consult a doctor about menopause.

Her life became a maelstrom of role overload, marital strife, and eventually the failure of her own business and ensuing lawsuits. Always trying to do more, like so many women, she paid little attention to the needs of her body. When she began to have panic attacks and tearful outbursts over the least little setback, she sought out a Chinese medicine practitioner. The diagnosis: early menopause. She was stunned.

"I'm a young mother—how can you even think I'm an old lady in menopause!" she demanded.

The practitioner explained that the combined demands of a late pregnancy and stressful life events had taken a toll. Her metabolism had become very slow and her hormone level increasingly unbalanced. The depressed woman did not want to accept this reality. She insisted that her problems must be related to PMS, and that she'd always had them in milder form. She went on running on empty.

This is not an uncommon story today. The juxtaposition of a late pregnancy and early menopause can make the transition more psychologically painful, because it is so abrupt.

Sex and the Change-of-Life Lover

*O*ne subject women are least likely to bring up in connection with menopause is any change in sexual interest. The raging hormones of adolescence may suddenly become the unraging hormones of menopause. Or, it may go exactly the other way.

For example, a high-profile movie executive I know went through a major career move in her late forties, the sort of jump that inevitably kicks up gossip: *Was she fired?* One of her best friends warned her: "You know, this could be a very bad mark on your career because people will say, 'She's probably postmenopausal.' You lose your value."

"What are you saying!" The executive gasped in disbelief. "A dried-up, over-the-hill, nasty old me? Do you really think that could be the perception out there?" From a distance, clad in a T-shirt, jeans, and Top-Siders, the slim blond woman could still be mistaken for fourteen.

"Well, you *are* getting older," warned the friend, probably projecting her own menopausal malaise.

"I was flushed with rage," admits the executive. "Because that meant I might be perceived as having no power." She began brooding on her mother's experience. From family pictures she remembered that her mother had been "cute" in her early fifties, but later in that decade, all at once, "her whole face died." So the executive had been spending more time on maintenance: getting her hair highlighted more frequently, going for collagen shots, doing a lot of "teeth things," dropping weight at a ritzy spa. Her first line of defense, she decided, would be to maintain her sex appeal and sexual energy.

"What's amazing is that at age fifty I'm having the best sex I've ever had," she told me confidently. Following a recent divorce, "that part of me has suddenly come to life." What does this have to do with menopause? Everything. Here is a woman who associates sexual potency with power, just like the men who have been her mentors and models at the top of corporate life.

"I made up my mind I'm not going to lose this part," she said fervently. Menopause *will* be held at bay as long as she can keep up her sexual élan.

In general, it can be said that women who enjoyed a lively sex life when they were younger are likely to go on enjoying—or missing—sex after menopause. Some psychoanalysts like Graciella Abelin-Sas, a member of the New York Psychoanalytic Institute, hear a common confession from their female patients over fifty: "I've never been as aware of my sexual urges in my whole life." Dr. Abelin says, "Women are ashamed of this. The myth of aging has conditioned them to believe that their sexuality should be going down the drain. They often feel that they are the exception, and they are embarrassed about being so sexual." As their mate's potency declines, or they become widowed or divorced, some women over fifty seen by psychiatrists are turning to homosexual relationships with other women, which they had never considered before. "The female mates are more loving, and more accepting of the physical changes," says Dr. Abelin.

"Most women after the menopause, if they're reasonably healthy and happy, do not experience a diminution in sex drive," says Dr. Ramey, the senior physiologist at Georgetown University. "But a very large number do—maybe 30 percent," she estimates, adding that the figures are unreliable because doctors don't ask women about their sex drive. "Since we're all living longer, this large number of women who face a diminished sex drive can be a very serious matter."

It is particularly startling for women who have always been sensual to find even slight changes in intimate pleasures they have taken for granted. Gayle Sand is a case in point. A slinky, sexy-looking California woman with great black Diana Ross hair, she flew all the way to Manhattan to have her bone density measured at the Osteoporosis Center at the Hospital for Special Surgery—that's how jittery she was about this thing called menopause.

"I've always been a person that's looked much younger than I actually was. Even now I don't think I look forty-nine years old, do I?" She leaned back in the mean metal institutional chair, attempting a seductive nonchalance, and let the strap of her laminated white tank top drop off one deeply tanned shoulder at the two o'clock point, precisely where the swell of breast tissue started to come up off her ribs. Not an ounce of fat was discernible on her body, nor was there a line apparent in her face. But inside, she was miserable.

"I've always taken really good care of myself. Look, it's like baby skin," she said, holding out an arm glistening like a peeled peach. She was proud of having a DNA glow—all from a diet of boneless, skinless sardines she read about in the Seventies in Cosmopolitan.

So what was she doing in an osteoporosis clinic, with all those brittle women suffering from low bone mass who have smoked and been slothful about exercise? Well, Sand's own mother had broken her pelvis. But we're not going to be like our mothers, are we? Sand belongs to the first generation of the new fifties woman. She has exercised almost every day of her life. "So I figured I'd postpone all of this. It wouldn't even get to me. The first time I even thought about it was in an exercise class at Sportsclub-L.A. Dyan Cannon, Teri Garr, Magic Johnson, they all go there—it's the stars' gym. I see the tushies of everyone. There's hardly a woman there who has her own breasts. And you can be sure none of *them* ever had *menopause*."

She was near the end of class, on the floor, grinding the old lower abs into the ground with leg lifts, when she started to perspire profusely. She thought, *What a great teacher!* "But later in the afternoon I was in Gelsons—it's, like, one of the best supermarkets in L.A.—and I started to have that feeling again. Oh-oh, maybe it wasn't just the great instructor." *Dorian Gray time! You're going to catch me being old.*

Sand was a dental hygienist: "I cleaned the teeth of the stars." She also had a new man in her life, a husband-to-be. She was in her psychiatrist's office when another hot flash hit, so she asked him about it. "If I were you," he said, "I would never mention menopause to this man." She followed the shrink's advice and hid her little secret from the man she married, which wasn't easy once she started having the night sweats.

Just beyond REM sleep—*bolt!*—she'd pop up like burnt toast. A minute later the sweating would start from every pore. Swiftly and silently she'd slip out from under the sheets and take a cold sponge bath, but sometimes her husband would awake and grumble, "Hey, it's wet in here! Jesuschrise, whatsammatta with these *sheets?*"

"I'm just having a little anxiety," she'd say, rubbing his head.

"But then around the same time your vagina starts to get dry. Also, I felt no desire." Now she was talking about a flagging of libido as the estrogen level drops and the tissues of the vaginal wall becomes thinner and drier. Imagine discussing *that* with your mate, said Sand. "Unless you have a really decent guy, talking to him about menopause is like taking hemlock."

She had learned from reading *Lear's* that yoga was the basis of Raquel Welch's regimen for reaching "balance, calmness, and energy." Of course, Raquel Welch, who at fifty looks like a low-fat-yogurt Lachaise, never mentions menopause. But Raquel does say the secret of remaining a sex symbol forever is yoga. "Change excites me. I am fifty years old. It's when the mind catches up with the body." Along with a diet of Evian water, oat bran, and protein-packed steamed salmon—that's all there is to it!

So Sand slid into bed as if she still belonged to a world of perfectly matched D-cup mango breasts and record arousal times, convinced that all she needed to do to enter the state of fifty-year-old erotica—the state of Raquel-mindedness—was "the mere act of holding a position for a count of thirty or forty seconds." She was thinking, *I'll be a menopause centerfold. I have this glistening body, right?* At the peak of a hot flash—*you want a hot woman? This is a hot woman.* Her new husband maneuvered her into position. And then, *it* hurt.

"It's hard to decide which came first, not wanting to have sex, or not wanting it because it hurt," said Sand.

Finally she sat her husband down and told him the facts of life. "I'm going through my Change of Life." Blank look. "I'm going through menopause." Her husband gave her a new name: My Change-of-Life Beauty Queen. She winced; it was a kiss with a kick.

"We find there's a definite major change in sexual response from premenopause to perimenopause," concludes Professor Phyllis Mansfield from her past studies. "Hormones primarily regulate sexual desire in human females," points out Dr. Kim Wallen, the primates researcher at Emory University. "Among monkeys, what we could call middle-aged females are the most socially savvy and attractive to males, and sex is primarily initiated by the female." When the researcher removed half of the estrogen they produce, some of the female monkeys continued to be sexually active, but when he removed all the estrogen, they lost all interest in sex.

Virtually the same phenomenon has been demonstrated at McGill University in studies of women aged thirty to fifty whose ovaries had been surgically removed. Whether or not they took estrogen orally after surgery, they were less interested, less aroused, and had fewer fantasies about sex. But while clinicians collect plenty of data on the frequency of intercourse, they seldom look at the key variable for females: sexual desire.

"There is an overall tendency among doctors to discount women's emotional needs," observes Dr. Wallen. "They will spend a lot of time seeing if there's vaginal atrophy, but they won't spend any time asking about sexual interest or enjoyment." This issue is still not seen as an appropriate part of a menopause workup. Yet a single woman without a regular sexual partner faces a different menopause from the married woman, since the former must be motivated if she is to find a mate.

Postmenopausal women who come into the McGill University menopause clinic in Montreal, Canada, often say, "The kids are gone, my husband and I like each other, we do lots more things together now. But I find I'm simply not interested in sex. Maybe I don't really love him." Certain women notice the falloff in desire quite suddenly, reports Barbara Sherwin, associate professor of psychology in the university's obstetrics-gynecology department and codirector of the clinic. "When I can date it to the onset of menopause or several years thereafter, or to surgical menopause, in women who didn't have that complaint before, we suspect what they are missing is testosterone."

Scientific measurements have established that the testosterone level goes down by about one-third in the average postmenopausal woman who still has her ovaries. If her ovaries are removed, the fall is twice as great. The figures come from an acknowledged expert in hormone measurement, Dr. Howard Judd.

"Every woman has been told, 'Don't worry, your adrenals take over,' but the point is, the adrenals don't take over," insists Dr. Lila Nachtigall of NYU. The adrenal glands make about two thirds of the testosterone circulating in the body of young women. But from the age of thirty on, a woman's adrenal glands slow down. Preliminary studies by Dr. Nachtigall show that after the ovaries are removed or shut down in postmenopause, the adrenal glands produce very little testosterone. What they do make is mostly in fat tissue of the body. "So if the woman is thin, she also has less testosterone," notes Dr. Sherwin.

In some proportion of postmenopausal women the ovaries go on overtime—producing more testosterone even than during their reproductive life. These are the women who notice an increased sex drive; some will develop an enlarged clitoris. They may also see some hair appearing on their upper lips or chin; or a slight recession of hair at the temples; or a deepening voice. A woman who wonders about her testosterone level can have it measured from a blood sample; good norms exist. But she would have to ask for it.

Fay Weldon, the novelist known internationally for her wickedly wry chronicles of the battle between the sexes, observes in her recent novel Life Force, ". . . when estrogen levels sink in a woman, it is safe for society to give her hormone-replacement therapy, which keeps a female soft, sweet, and smiling, but antisocial to give the aging man testosterone injections, for if you do he runs round raping women and hitting other men on the head. What a bummer!" In the novel four women of a certain age are revisited by the same old lover, Leslie of the Magnificent Dong, who is sixty years old but still intent upon using his vital ten inches to revive infidelities of the past . . . "leaping, unstoppable, like electricity, from this one to that one, burning us up, making us old," as one of his menopausal targets describes the experience. But testosterone for women? The intriguing possibilities hadn't yet occurred to Weldon. One can't wait to see what her imagination might do with that new wrinkle.

I visited Weldon in the leafy Kentish Town section of London. A great blond Valkyrie of a woman, feet planted firmly in the earth of her tiny townhouse garden, she was waiting outside to welcome me. We threaded our way through her sun-splashed work parlor, past a grown son slumped in a beanbag sofa on the phone, and into a small solarium. All around were bunches of beautiful, blowsy late-summer roses, their petals splayed wide open, a rather apt simile for the attractive Earth Mother who sat before me.

In her mid-fifties, Weldon still sees sex as a necessary indulgence that both men and women need to survive. "I suppose, by and large, men have more opportunity to be sexually active as they grow older," she told me, "but I think women remain more sexually alive."

There is an important and poignant exception to this view. It's what Germaine Greer is trying to get at when she talks about having rejected hormone replacement. "When I used it myself, I didn't like that feeling of going back into the cycle," she said in an interview on CNN. She had already been postmenopausal for a while, and having "glimpsed another place" beyond sexual desire, she "wanted to get back there."

If a woman no longer feels competitive or graceful in the guise of sexual huntress, she might well take the attitude, "Good riddance, who needs men?" The argument against hormone replacement then comes from an entirely new orientation: Life without sex can be more peaceful and allow one to get more done. And, in truth, it may make some women happier than continuing along in the same state of emotional frenzy—open to humiliation, rejection, anxiety, and misery as well as to the pleasures of sex. The woman's underlying fear here is that after a certain age, her face can't be saved, her body is going, and she can't find a man. If one then takes the position that all men are beasts or sexually inferior, there is no need to admit that one doesn't really enjoy sex.

This may explain in part why some women start replacing their hormones and then stop. While they were not circulating much of their own hormones, desire may have slowly ebbed. One doesn't really notice. But if it's restimulated by taking hormones, one realizes that there is always another level of sexual tension that runs along underneath, rendering one vulnerable to expectation and disappointment. Once it's back, and she is an older woman, her options are to satisfy it or to sustain an inconsolable longing. Throwing out the pills or patches, then, may have less to do with sore breasts or feeling puffy than the need to take herself out of play. Otherwise, she opens herself to hurt again. It's not easy to put one's finger on it, because the vulnerability is not just to sexual longing. It is opening oneself again to the possibility of being in love.

"Do I have to accept this?" is a question increasingly being asked by dynamic women in their fifties who are at the peak of their careers but alarmed to find their sexual pilot light abruptly lowered. Treatment with very small amounts of testosterone—always combined with estrogen —is beginning to be popular.

Adding a testosterone preparation to estrogen replacement improves well-being and energy levels, especially in surgically menopausal women. It also revives sex drive and, often, cognitive functioning. More important, while estrogen alone stops additional bone loss, testosterone preparations help to rebuild depleted bone. Physicians and scientists are trying to determine if testosterone is necessary to maintain female muscle mass and bone density into old age. They are divided over the wisdom of giving postmenopausal women small doses of testosterone along with the estrogen-replacement therapy they may receive. Although recent evidence is mixed, doctors worry that testosterone may negatively affect cholesterol, thus raising the risk of heart disease.

Dr. Barbara Sherwin, who has been conducting research on estrogen-testosterone combinations for fifteen years at McGill University, has had women on this combination of drugs, by injection, for up to twenty years with good results. She cautions that with a full dose of testosterone about 20 percent developed some facial hair. When she cut the dose in half, to 75 mg of testosterone once a month, less than five percent of women had any side effects. When given by injection, testosterone had no effect on HDL and LDL cholesterol levels. But it had a powerful effect on restoring libido and well-being in women who have had hysterectomies and who produce very little of their own testosterone.

Testing for testosterone levels is expensive (around $100) and usually unnecessary. Even if results show a woman has "normal" levels of hormone, those levels may be insufficient in her particular case. Dr. Gloria Bachmann, chief of the division of general obstetrics and gynecology at the University of Medicine and Dentistry of New Jersey, cautions that testosterone preparations should only be given as a component of HRT when there is a clear indication. "Many women will experience relief from estrogens (or estrogen-progesterone) alone. If after three months response is inadequate, a trial with androgens [testosterone] should be considered."

Dr. John Moran, a veteran British gynecologist who has treated thousands of menopausal women over the past fifteen years, recommends a very weak testosterone called ProViron. With one half to one tablet per day—much less than the dosage recommended by the standard medical handbook—there seem to be no masculinizing side effects, but there is a subtle return of sexual vitality.

"For those postmenopausal women who find themselves having difficulty with arousal and reaching orgasm, a small amount of testosterone can make a big difference," confirms Dr. Ramey. The one-thousand doctors at the 1993 meeting of the North American Menopause Society were asked to raise their hands if they were prescribing testosterone; 25 to 30 percent did.

When I checked back with Gayle Sand, she had been told by a female doctor about topical estrogen, a very low dose of Premarin used vaginally as a medication to maintain lubrication and keep tissue from thinning in the vaginal walls. "The effects were great," she exclaimed. "I have a normal sex life again." But she had also started a campaign to end the taboo. She'll speak up in an elevator: "Is it warm in here, or am I having a hot flash?" When the occupants gasp, giggle, then cluck, "You, you're too young for that," Sand sings back, "No, I'm not. I'm menopausal."

Over-the-counter preparations can restore moisture to the tissues of the vagina *without* the use of hormones. Gloria Bachmann, at the University of Medicine and Dentistry of New Jersey, along with Morris Notelovitz of the Women's Medical Center in Gainesville, Florida, conducted a one-year study demonstrating that Replens significantly increased vaginal health and quality of life in women suffering from vaginal dryness. The product works best when used on a continuous basis, rather than just prior to intercourse.

"By and large, the women who have a problem with

sexuality in middle life are old married women, like me," believes Janine O'Leary Cobb, editor of *A Friend Indeed*, the Canadian menopause newsletter. (Address: P.O. Box 1710, Champlain, NY 12919-1710.) "Many of us feel we had great sex when we were younger, and we don't mind if we have less now." But Cobb gets letters from women fifty and fifty-two who have taken new, younger lovers. "They're hot to trot and having a lovely time; sex was never so good."

Thus is born a new Old Wives' Tale, in which women pass the word about the tonic effect of a Change-of-Life Lover. The head of a department at a prestigious university was in her mid-forties when she first heard about it from a woman in her mid-fifties. The older woman told her to look forward to menopause: Pregnancy worries went out the window, and she'd had an affair of *grande passion* at that time— starting at forty-nine.

"I was stunned," recalls the younger woman. She is petite and had always prided herself on being taken for younger than she was, but the habit of marriage to a man she had known for several decades had made a buried treasure of her erotic self. Then, suddenly, she found herself swept up in an affair. When? She smacks her forehead with the insight: "It's only now I recognize I was the same age! Maybe I thought, *Forty-nine—last chance*."

Gloria Steinem, known not only as the inspiration of the American feminist movement but as one of the most sexually animated women of her time, was delightfully frank when I asked her what a fulfilling sex life means to her now, having passed fifty.

"I am about to say a series of things that if I had heard them ten years ago, I wouldn't have believed them." She laughed. "All the readers of this should brace themselves— just have faith that it may be true for them, too." She laughed again. "Sex and sensuality—going to bed for two entire days and sending out for Chinese food—was such an important part of my life, and it just isn't anymore. It's still there, but it's less important. I don't know how much of it is hormonal and how much is outgrowing it."

Her face seemed more relaxed. She lay back against her sofa cushions, this peripatetic woman who never in the last eighteen years spent more than a few days at a time in her own apartment, and she looked, at last, at home. "It doesn't really matter whether sex goes or doesn't go," she summed up. "What matters is that the older woman can choose whether it goes or not."

Carmen Callil, a high-powered London book publisher, chuckles when she thinks back on the "revolting promiscuity" that she and her generation of the feminist vanguard engaged in during the Sixties and Seventies. "I was obsessed with sex then," she admits. "But when you're younger, sex is about other things, too—adventure, boldness, identity." Like Steinem, she never married. "There's no doubt about it, I'm not as interested in sex as I used to be." Sex has taken a place in her postmenopausal life comparable to television. Nice, but if she has something better to do, not now.

In championing the embrace of "manlessness," Germaine Greer claims that half the women of menopausal age will be without a man in their bed anyway. This is a greatly exaggerated estimate. In the U.S. March 1990 National Census, the percentage of forty-five- to fifty-four-year-old women who were single, widowed, divorced, or married with a spouse absent totalled one quarter of their age group.

Happily married women or those who continue to enjoy having men in their lives cannot buy into militant celibacy. Newswoman Eve Pollard says, "For those of us who are trying to juggle nine lives, including a long-term relationship with a man, the idea that because you stop menstruating, you should pack it all in, is nonsensical. I would be the first one to say, if you're not terribly happy with this boring man and don't want to wash his socks, why wait till you have the menopause? Get out before. Who knows who you might meet?"

In sum, it may be vague melancholy, stimulated by the sexual aliveness revived by being on hormones, from which the physical symptoms are the excuse to withdraw. The very possibility of being open again to hurt causes some women, discarded or ignored by men, to say, "Why bother?" But in not bothering to revive their sexual desire, they may ignore caring for their bodies and mental well-being.

Educating Your Man

~

*M*ost men go all twitchy when mention is made of anything to do with female reproductive organs or processes. They don't want to hear about your visit to the gynecologist, and they'll do *anything* to get out of making a run to the 7-Eleven to pick up tampons. There seems to be a hangover from primitive thinking that presupposes a woman is unclean when she is in cycle. And if she has "female troubles," the last person she can count on for a supportive ear may be her man. Those deep inner spaces are supposed to be only for pleasuring; they are not meant to have clinical names or flesh-and-blood malfunctions.

Patriarchal and primitive societies have done their part in prescribing the menstrual taboo. Just as they have fostered a division of women into two dimensions—good little ovulating wife who is the passive receptacle, and the scarlet woman or witch, who is active, sexually dynamic, and terrifying—men in traditional cultures have isolated the menstruating woman as "unclean," "polluting," and "dangerous." One would logically think that the woman who is finished with the fearsome business of monthly bleeding would become better accepted, and in some traditional cultures she is. But there is a new, subjective fear, and not just in primitive societies.

Middle-aged men, as they themselves begin to slow down, have a good deal of fear and envy of the physical, mental, sexual, and spiritual energies of fully evolved women— women who are beyond being objects defined by the male gaze and now fully conscious keepers of their own bodies. That fear is projected back onto women, causing us to wonder if we really are over the hill when we no longer have value primarily as erotic objects and reliable breeders.

In fact, married men are more apprehensive about the effects of menopause on their life satisfaction than women themselves. In a 1991 Gallup Poll commissioned by Ciba-Geigy, makers of the Estraderm patch, one in four of the seven hundred women aged forty to sixty expressed concern about menopause, but two thirds of the middle-aged husbands were bothered about it. Only a third of the women were satisfied with their husband's knowledge about the Change of Life, and with good reason. Two thirds of the husbands of premenopausal women expressed fears that their sex lives would be compromised by having a wife in menopause. A majority of the men married to women in the transition focused on the emotional impact on their wives, saying the women manifested anxiety, irritability, and mood swings. Fewer than half the men took any notice of physical problems that underlay these emotional reactions, despite the fact that the overwhelming majority of the women in menopause reported struggling with hot flashes, night sweats, and difficulty sleeping.

A gynecological nurse at New York Hospital is struck by how men shun their wives when they come into the hospital for a hysterectomy. "The absence of the husband when it's an issue of female sex organs is so common," says Tanya Resilard. "And if they do come to visit, they seem afraid to go to the bedside. They want to be totally separate."

"My husband was incredibly supportive when I had breast cancer, but he really doesn't want to acknowledge I'm in menopause," I was told by a gutsy entertainer. Her spouse is a few years younger than she. When she tries to talk to him about having problems with concentration, he ascribes it to something else—it's stress or money problems or maybe flu—anything but the Change of Life. "He is in major denial about it—why?"

If you are getting older, so is your man. You may represent the mirror of his own aging. Breast cancer a husband can't catch. But aging is sex-neutral. Another woman who felt constrained about admitting to her husband she was struggling with menopause finally realized why. She was the second wife and represented to the husband his own renaissance. "He once told me, 'I don't ever want to think of you as middle-aged.'"

"In certain parts of the South they make you feel really shameful," notes Effie Graham, who grew up in Blanch, North Carolina, and is now a nurse's aide at New York Hospital. "The men refuse to let you sleep in the same room, tell you you're supposed to go through it alone. They had a lot of religious beliefs about menopause. They always said the Lord would take care of it."

As much as possible, it helps not to project one's own fears on the man. In fact, a woman can tell him there is much to recommend a woman nearing the end of her reproductive stage. With the passing of pregnancy fears, her lustier fantasies can be played out with a refreshing lack of inhibitions. Best of all—and she must boast about this—she is soon to be free of the "blue meanies" that come with monthly cycles. The Gallup Poll findings support this good news: Living through menopause puts far less strain on marriages than the apprehensions would suggest. A nearly identical majority of the husbands and wives polled—70 percent—acknowledged that, in fact, the women's interest in sex had not decreased during or after menopause. And two out of five of the women presently in the transition or just past it say that their relationship with their husbands has improved since menopause, while the majority of women reported the quality of their marriages has remained the same.

If there are physical problems or discomforts, they do need an honest airing. The consequences of not being honest with your man about what's going on can magnify the psychological burden and become devastating. Two middle-aged men came to hear a talk I gave on menopause at a health resort. I was delighted to see them in the audience but curious as to why they would join a group of fifty women. Each of them came to me in his own time to unburden himself.

"I had no idea what women go through in these years," said the trial lawyer, who later stretched beside me after a hike. "My wife may be silently suffering." He sounded seriously concerned, even abashed. "I'm going to talk to her about menopause as soon as I get home."

The other man, a New York lawyer, caught up with me as we were boarding the plane and seemed to need to talk. "I think men need to be educated about menopause even more than women," he said.

"Your wife is a lucky woman," I quipped. My remark set off a shudder of pain in his face, though he said nothing further. Later, over coffee, he told me that his wife had exhibited many of the symptoms I had described. "The sweating at night, insomnia, problems with concentrating. Her moods were up and down, and then mostly down. I had no idea what it was."

Further conversation revealed that his wife had lost her job as a teacher in the recession. Their son had moved out to his own apartment. And she had brought her mother up from Florida to care more attentively for her, but the frail woman had liver cancer and soon died. All in all, a rather typical portrait of the stresses of social as well as physical change many women experience during the menopausal years.

"I guess I just didn't stop to think how much these losses meant to her. And on top of it, the drain of menopause," he said, flooded with guilt. I tried to comfort him and suggest new approaches for the future. It was too late. One day, four months before, his wife had driven him to their suburban train station for his commute to the city. She knew he had a late dinner with the senior partner that night. When he came home, he noticed the window of the garage door milky. He found his wife entombed in the car.

The
Menopause
Gateway

~

$\mathcal{S}$ome women have genetic good fortune. Even after entering menopause, they continue to make enough female hormone precursors in their adrenal glands, and to make enough estrogen from these precursors in their fat deposits, so that they experience no symptoms at all or, at most, only temporary hot flashes. This pause is a marker event in their lives, but it does not take on the physical or psychological freight of a major event.

"They are thrilled not to have to deal with the menstrual cycle anymore, and some of them seem to maintain their bone levels very well," observes Theresa Galsworthy, the nurse-clinician who directs the Osteoporosis Center at the Hospital for Special Surgery in New York. Broad-scale figures on the proportion of women who fall into this fortunate group are probably impossible to come by, but activity at the Osteoporosis Center offers a clue. "During the course of the week about fifteen patients come to me to have their bone density measured because they're fairly newly postmenopausal. Maybe two or three of the fifteen have absolutely no symptoms," says Galsworthy. These women are usually on the older side of the norm when they experience the Change, fifty-one or fifty-two.

Women who deal with menopause by denying it entirely become easy to pick out. They are the ones you see eating a lettuce leaf and glass of seltzer for lunch, their hair color slightly lurid, their time more and more taken up with becoming skillful makeup artists or searching for the right cosmetic surgeon. The results may be admirable and mask the years, but sooner or later time and nature will catch up with us all.

Strenuous dieting at this age, for instance, is the worst way to preserve one's long-term health and grace. Estrogen is stored in the body's fat cells. Some researchers differenti-ate between the Thin Woman's Menopause and the Plump Woman's Menopause, the latter usually being far less symptomatic. "In populations where women don't get car-ried away with wearing a size six dress when they're fifty-five, and they still do regular exercise and they're not smoking, bone fractures are not much of a problem," says Dr. Elizabeth L. Barrett-Connor, a top epidemiologist at the University of California, San Diego.

At the opposite extreme are women who allow them-selves to become "victims" of menopause, using this time of life as an excuse to become inactive, go to fat, beg off sex, and sulk, often leading them to depression and the door of menopause clinics. These are the middle-aged women who perpetuate the stereotype of the menopausal woman as synonymous with "mean old bitch."

The professional women I have studied are accustomed to considerable control over their environment, and they have worked hard to achieve it. They pride themselves on being fiercely organized and prepared for just about any crisis. These mid-forties dynamos can fax a dinner menu to a caterer, sell a stock, talk supportively to a spouse over a portable phone without missing a step, and remember to take their aerobics shoes to the office along with their satin slingbacks so they'll be able to exercise before appearing glamorous at the AIDS benefit—all this on the way to do cancer surgery. But they cannot control when they break out in a hot flash or when they bleed.

The meanest loss of menopause, for them, is the sudden loss of control. Among high-performing professionals, puzzlement often develops into panic followed by outrage. That was the route traveled by Meredith, a mother of two and model business leader in her middle-American community, who had stopped counting birthdays at thirty-eight. That was the year she went into business and consciously knew she looked terrific and felt the same way.

She started having mysterious migraines at forty-two. They grew more frequent. Over the next ten years she traipsed around to one gynecologist after another, all of whom posited psychological causes—i.e., "Type A's are often migrainous." At age fifty Meredith was the one to insist upon a blood test that would measure her hormones. She had zero estrogen and zero progesterone. Now completely frustrated, she saw a TV commercial for a menopause clinic in Cleveland, Ohio. She flew there to have a bone densitometer test, which revealed she had 10 percent less bone mass than the norm for women her age. Not one doctor up to then had mentioned her bones in connection with menopause or brought up the risk of osteoporosis.

"I feel like I dropped a percentage point of bone mass in each one of those doctors' offices," Meredith says ruefully. She also wonders, with good reason, if the migraines were the result of estrogen depletion over the past ten years.

I recognized her immediately when we first met. It was the walk, perhaps. Her long legs took the sidewalk one full paving stone at a time, high heels notwithstanding. She was good-looking, still blond and pink-complexioned, the parentheses at either side of her mouth lending animation to her face. Her friends had described her as "dynamic, tough, successful, and doesn't take no for an answer." Her real estate company will do 55 million dollars of business this year, and her mortgage banking company will do 80 million.

"You'd think I could manage my period, right?" Meredith wisecracked. Fifty—the number itself—held no menace for her, she said, although it came out that the year Meredith turned fifty, her mother died of breast cancer. It was her first personal experience with death, immediately followed by the onset of menopause. "And something happened to me, I don't know what, I became a little nutsy about flying in an airplane. I began to feel a foreshortening of time." Meredith said she was too busy to figure it out.

"I've been obsessed," she says. "Menopause is the only thing that's made me feel I had an age. Because I can't get rid of it. I hate it, big time."

During a group interview, Meredith held up the computerized cost-benefit chart she had designed to analyze whether or not to take hormone replacement therapy. The impressive-looking graph was all the more infuriating to her because there was no bottom line. "So what do I go for? Cancer, osteoporosis, or heart disease?"

For her, menopause represents her lack of control over mortality. Most of us don't have to face up to mortality until our mothers die. The loss of that unconditional love leaves no cushion between ourselves and the outrages of life, no grip against a suddenly perceived slippage on "the downward path" toward one's own inevitable "dusty death." Control becomes magnified in importance. In reaction, Meredith developed her new phobia about airplanes, where as a passenger she could exercise no control. Still, she had pushed away any conscious recognition of her own aging until the physical insults of menopause finally made it impossible to remain, even in her own mind, thirty-eight.

Now, faced with making a medical decision about her own life that involves the breast cancer issue, with the loss of her mother not yet mourned, Meredith is in a constant state of conflict. She longs to escape from her own success: "Being a mentor is a burden. I feel like I don't live anything new." She resents her husband's assumption that he will take early retirement. " 'What about me?' I feel like saying. 'When can I retire?' " She is unconsciously afraid that she will follow her mother before she has had time to live fully. All these fears and frustrations have been focused on the secondary issue of menopause. And they come out as anger.

To make matters more frustrating, the cost-benefit analysis on how to treat menopause resists adding up to any clear, rational, risk-free answer. Why? Because we don't have enough data. And because everything has a price. A well-informed, affluent woman like Meredith might well decide, "Well, hell, if I know hormones are going to protect my heart, my mind, and my bones, I guess I can monitor my breasts with mammography and my uterus with ultrasound, and see how it goes." Or she may prefer to try to manage the whole process naturally.

Partnering Yourself Through a Natural Menopause

～

$\mathcal{M}$any women resist medicalizing a natural event such as the Change. Others, like Serafina Corsello, have little choice.

"I had a wonderful defense, called denial," admits Dr. Corsello, an elegant European woman who practices nutritional medicine at the Corsello Center on Manhattan's West Side. She was simply never going to have all those unseemly symptoms other women report, poor things. Blessed with high energy and an insatiable desire for learning beyond dogma, Corsello completed a medical internship and residency in New York. Throughout her thirties she juggled a classical medical practice with being a single mother. But in her early forties she became disenchanted with mainstream medicine. The outcome of her midlife crisis was a commitment to educate herself in complementary medicine—vitamin therapy and other natural procedures—realizing that it meant she would have to study every day for the rest of her life.

"Will I be able to keep up this level of performance?" she worried as she plunged into self-education, taking on new financial burdens as well as committing to a second marriage. But at fifty she found she still had fantastic energy, having always been able to hit the pillow and sleep within two seconds.

"At fifty-two all of a sudden I'd hit the pillow, and hit the pillow—at two in the morning I'd still be hitting the pillow. This was the first sign; it was devastating."

It took Dr. Corsello no time to get an estrogen patch and congratulate herself on reregulating her sleep. She was herself again for the next two years. "One day I woke up and felt an ominous mass in my breast." The large cyst made her suddenly aware of the history of cancer in her family. She looked at her lovely little patch and synthetic progesterone pills and said, "Adieu, chérie."

She doctored herself with Chinese herbs, indulged in a massage once a week, and concentrated on creating a new aesthetic in her life. She surrounds herself with classical music, even in her office it is constantly in the background, soothing her. Since she loathes exercise but loves dancing, Dr. Corsello built in her own unique daily stress-reducing activity. She shuts the bedroom door while she watches a tape of the *MacNeil/Lehrer NewsHour* and throws herself into high-paced disco dancing, all by herself.

At age fifty-eight, vivacious and utterly charming, Serafina Corsello signed a ten-year lease on her office in Manhattan—a powerful statement of her belief that "I'm not only in my prime now, but I'm on my way up." Like many professional women, she is operating under a different time line from her male peers. Her career development was delayed by single motherhood and slowed slightly by menopause. "I cannot stop at sixty because I have hardly begun," she says enthusiastically. But there is nothing stopping her now. She works every day, and on weekends she studies and writes. "The constant intellectual stimulation allows my mind and body to remain attuned. I keep on improving," she says.

The greatest reward of fifty-plus years of experience, she finds, is mental efficiency. She can actually sense her right and left brains, working in synchrony. And with this wide spectrum of intellectual capacity, she says, "We can zoom in to get the whole picture." She now expresses her ideas on health care *without fear* of offending the male medical establishment. She no longer labors under the younger woman's apprehensions—"What if I'm not right?" or, "Oh, my God, will they be offended?"

"Do you know how much energy this saves?" she says, twinkling. "I used to go into preambles—'you know' and 'on the other hand'—but I've cut fifty percent of that—it's freedom!" As she says now, "If I'm not right, well, I'm not right. This attitude allows you to shortcut all the tangents you had to go through as a young woman—because no longer being a sexual object, you're no longer trying to *please* anybody. At this point what is important to me is elegance. And elegance has nothing to do with sex." The greatest change she has noticed is the aesthetic confidence she has developed as an older woman.

Dr. Corsello has explored most of the herbal preparations popularly used to ease menopausal symptoms. She finds the most effective to be dong quai, a Chinese herbal remedy. "If I'm under stress, bingo, I take thirty or forty little drops and find miraculous relief." She suggests a woman ask a Chinese herbalist to make up a mixture to suppress hot flashes.

Dong quai, the Chinese herb, contains plant sterols that have estrogenlike effects. Plant estrogens are estimated to be one four-hundredth as strong as the estrogen from pregnant mare's urine found in Premarin. Dong quai is available in health food stores in capsules, liquid, or as teas. Siberian ginseng is possibly helpful in opposing fatigue and depressive symptoms. It, too, is available in health food stores, or easily taken as ginseng tea.

The theory in Chinese medicine is that energy in the kidneys begins to decline for women around the age of forty-nine, and so it was written in the ancient Chinese texts. Today, a practitioner would assess the individual woman and make up a mixture of herbs to revitalize her kidney function. Dr. Denning Cai, a highly experienced Chinese medicine doctor in Tarzana, California, sees many high-profile women in the Los Angeles area who are so terrified of menopause, they actually bring it on themselves earlier.

"People with an aggressive personality—women who try so hard to reach something, who feel 'I have to,' and who push themselves hard all the time—put the body under higher stress," Dr. Cai observes, "and this can bring on the menopause sooner." If she works with such women early enough to rebalance and calm their bodies, sometimes the menopause is delayed.

The Indian homeopathic tradition, as practiced by the world-renowned Shyam S. Singha, who has several clinics in London and one in Suffolk, is to treat menopause entirely through diet and homeopathic remedies. He finds the agnus castus herb particularly helpful in rebalancing estrogen and progesterone levels. He also recommends dolomite, a mineral rich in magnesium and calcium. Almonds, soaked overnight and peeled, are also very rich in calcium.

Vitamin E is commonly used to relieve hot flashes. Primrose oil is another long-standing remedy. It contains gamma-linolenic acid, which helps mediate hormonal activity. Women who frequent the health spa at Rancho la Puerta volunteered that acupuncture once a month has helped them with hot flashes and night sweats that disturb sleep as well as with alleviating dry vagina.

The most helpful modifications you can make in your diet are:

1. Low fat.
2. High calcium.

3. Increase the tofu in your diet (but tofu is high in fat, so it has to be balanced out). You can make mayonnaise or salad dressing out of tofu or use it with yogurt as a vegetable dip.

4. Eat yams—a source of natural plant estrogen. Yams also have lots of beta-carotene in them, which is an antioxidant and will help support your immune system.

The best natural defense against osteoporosis is to keep the acidity of your blood in proper balance. If you don't, your body will, by removing calcium from your bones to defend the pH balance in the blood. Blood acidity is caused, first and foremost, by chronic stress. Therefore, it is of the utmost importance for any woman over forty-five, faced with high-stress professional or personal demands, to commit herself to some restorative relaxation measure. It might be biofeedback, prayer, yoga, or routine meditation.

I find much wisdom in the ancient Hindu health system known as Ayurveda. The guiding principle is that any disorder can be prevented as long as balance is maintained, in the mind and spirit as well as in the body. Dr. Deepak Chopra, one of the first M.D.'s to introduce Ayurvedic theory and practice in the West, explains in his book *Perfect Health:* "The mind exerts the deepest influence on the body, and freedom from sickness depends upon contacting our own awareness, bringing it into balance, and then extending that balance to the body. This state of balanced awareness, more than any kind of physical immunity, creates a higher state of health."

From modern science we know that the hypothalamus, or "the brain's brain," is responsible for balancing everything that goes on automatically in the body. Less than an ounce of gray matter in the forebrain, the hypothalamus must simultaneously balance the body's temperature, rate of metabolism, and sleep, along with its growth, hunger, thirst, blood chemistry, respiration, and many other functions. For optimum health to be maintained, coordination by the hypothalamus must be as precise as the movements of a conductor with a 150-piece orchestra.

During the perimenopause and early phase of menopause, even the brain's brain is often thrown off by the unpredictable changes in a woman's internal hormonal milieu. Try as it might, sending desperate signals to the pituitary gland to activate more estrogen, the hypothalamic regulator is confused when the ovaries don't respond as they did before. It can't do its usual conducting job. Hence, the body is often out of balance. Good health is harder to maintain.

Many women will develop allergies for the first time during the menopausal transition. If the state of imbalance is allowed to become too extreme, and the immune system is weakened, a disease process sets in. Everyone recognizes the sensations that presage an upcoming cold or flu, even though they are vague. Similarly, a menopausal woman whose body is seriously out of balance will feel "out of sorts," tired, cranky, and may complain of vague discomforts that are the body's premonition of disease.

Most doctors are baffled or impatient with such reports (if a woman even thinks her complaints serious enough to take to a doctor). Unless a woman takes herself seriously, and invests some time in learning about her vulnerabilities at this time of life, she may wind up in illness.

What can you do for yourself? The single most important aid to continued health through the menopausal transition is proper rest. When you feel that you are pushing yourself too hard or racing, stop and rest if only for five minutes. Even better, learn how to meditate. The most restful rest, aside from a night's sleep, is the deep relaxation experienced during the state of meditation. According to Dr. Chopra, the common symptoms of the "worried well" in menopause—headache, insomnia, low-level anxiety or depression—benefit most from the act of meditation. One can emerge thoroughly settled and refreshed after only a few minutes of transcending.

It is not wise to drink alcohol or too much coffee while you are trying to rebalance your body. Moreover, to minimize loss of mineral from bone it is vital to keep the acidity level in your blood as low as possible. Smoking, alcohol, and coffee also raise acid levels in the blood. Even a nightly glass of wine can wreak havoc with a hormonal system already out of balance. Carbonated sodas and beef, both of which have a high phosphorus content, are particularly dangerous for postmenopausal women, advises Dr. Corsello. She suggests a diet that emphasizes vegetables, complex carbohydrates, fiber, fish, and vegetable proteins such as tofu.

No natural remedies can be guaranteed effective, and none, of course, is approved by the FDA. Bear in mind that no pharmaceutical company stands to cash in on herbal remedies, since they are natural and can be sold over the counter. And since drug companies fund much of the medical research, it is not surprising that there is no serious money going into the study of Chinese medicine and its impact on menopause.

The pledge to have a "natural menopause," while politically correct, presents some contradictions. Is it "natural" to live for decades beyond fifty? And to want to feel in our seventies the way we do now?

This will be the first generation to get old routinely, and one way or another its women will have to provide some things that mother nature did not. None of the herbal remedies protects against bone loss. Janet Zand, a Chinese medical practitioner in Los Angeles, claims that herbs can diminish atrophy of the vagina. But as estrogen levels decline, the vaginal tissues become thinner and dryer.

Gradually, over the decade of menopause, the vagina will shrink in both length and width. One female gynecologist drew me a picture of the normal estrogenized vagina of a woman in her thirties. It looked about five inches long and the width of two middle fingers.

"In many women of sixty who have taken no estrogen, I can hardly insert my pinkie," said the gynecologist. If a woman discontinues hormone-replacement, the process of atrophy will start again. Doctors recommend that older women keep up an active sex life because that will keep the vaginal walls elastic. But the common reason that women don't "use it" and eventually "lose it" is that making love becomes naturally painful when the vagina shrinks in size. Estrogen cream, as explained, and new over-the-counter preparations do counteract the discomfort.

The Hidden Thieves

*A*ctive women often take pride in toughing it out: "I was too busy to notice menopause—I just sailed right through it" is their refrain. They may not be fully aware of the hidden thieves of menopause: osteoporosis, cognitive changes, and heart disease. This knowledge must be factored in before any of us can make an intelligent decision about how best to manage our own menopause.

Start up a conversation with any group of women where the ratio of blond to gray has tipped well over the fifty-fifty standoff, and there will be one woman who proclaims righteously, "Hormones. Not me! I want to stay healthy." Another will insist smugly, "I love my estrogen, I wouldn't give it up for anything!" And another will be totally ambivalent, able to be talked into either decision. Elizabeth Barrett-Connor, the University of California epidemiologist, observes that women break down into these three camps.

Most women have become phobic about breast cancer, with some good reason. Their fear, however, leaves them vulnerable to a greater threat. At each group interview I asked the participants to guess what they were most likely to die from. The answers always startled me. Nine out of ten women will say cancer, most of them specifying breast cancer. A few will throw in the possibilities of airline or auto crashes. Almost no one mentions the number one killer of women over fifty.

Heart disease.

In fact, *a woman's chances of dying from heart disease is more than double that of dying from cancer of any kind.* Even as the rise in breast cancer among American women continues apace—one in *nine* women is now diagnosed, and one in four of those will die from breast cancer within five years—cardiovascular disease quietly kills off one in *two* women over the age of fifty.

The Cheating Heart

*M*enopause increases the risk of coronary artery disease. And as the arteries get smaller, the chance of a heart attack becomes greater. Although the risk of heart attack does not increase abruptly at the moment a woman reaches natural menopause, the rate of heart disease does rise sharply over the course of the decade after a woman reaches her fifties. (Strokes have nothing to do with menopause.) A clear picture of the "cumulative, absolute risks" of the major causes of death for white women—between the ages of fifty and ninety-four—were spelled out in an editorial accompanying the Nurses' Health Study. There is a 31 percent absolute risk of dying of heart disease, a 2.8 percent risk of dying of breast cancer, a 2.8 percent risk of a hip fracture, and only a 0.7 percent risk of uterine cancer.

"Then why don't we read about women having heart attacks the way we do men?" someone will sensibly demand.

Perhaps because doctors pay less attention to women's symptoms of heart disease and treat them less aggressively than they do men. As a result, women often develop more advanced heart disease and are more likely to have fatal heart attacks than men. Two new studies involving tens of thousands of patients have recently shown irrefutable evidence of sex differences in the way heart conditions are treated. The unawareness of the general public simply reflects the prevailing attitude in the medical fraternity that heart disease is a man's disease.

"Women lag behind men in heart disease by about five to seven years," says Dr. Trudy Bush. "It really starts hitting women in their late fifties and sixties." By the age of sixty-seven they are just as likely to have a heart attack as their husbands, but more likely to die from it.

The most significant predictor of heart disease is the HDL level. Bad cholesterol levels normally increase in women for some ten to fifteen years following the cessation of periods. Again, dangerous changes in cholesterol count or blood pressure do not announce themselves with obvious symptoms, not until there is a medical catastrophe. "If your HDL level is low, and your LDL level is relatively higher—even if you're walking around with a total cholesterol count of 200—you're going to be in trouble," says Dr. Ramey. Estrogen replacement therapy decreases LDL (bad) cholesterol levels by about 15 percent and raises the HDL (good) cholesterol levels by the same amount.

Estrogen has a direct effect on the wall of the blood vessels. "Cholesterol uptake is the first change that occurs in the creation of the plague that forms the basis for heart disease," explains Dr. Lindsay. "Estrogen appears to block that effect, resulting in open vessels and good blood flow." That explains why estrogen reduces heart disease.

The Nurses' Health Study, the first prospective study of women's health with a population of tens of thousands of women (almost exclusively white), has found striking results on the heart disease front. After ten years, 48,000 of the subjects—who had no histories of cancer or heart disease when the study began—were evaluated. "Women who were taking estrogen, after menopause, had just half as many heart attacks and deaths [from heart attacks] as women who never used estrogen," reported Meir Stampfer, who led the study. An evaluation by Dr. Lee Goldman of Brigham and Women's Hospital in Boston concludes, "The benefits of estrogen outweigh the risks, substantially."

If your goal is to lower your risk of heart disease, you may want to take hormone therapy indefinitely. The recently reported PEPI trial adds to the already impressive evidence from the Nurses' Health Study: Again, estrogen cut the potential of cardiovascular disease among women in *half*. It also reduces by 50 percent their risk of dying from a heart attack. Among older women, age 65 to 74, a newer study found a 30 percent lower death rate from heart disease if the woman had taken estrogen for at least ten years. Most of the benefits lingered even in older women no longer taking the drugs.

For women who have had a hysterectomy, the most beneficial postmenopausal therapy is using estrogen alone. At last, after a half-century of conflicting data, Dr. Healy confirms, "We can confidently assert that estrogen reduces key cardiovascular risk factors in women at a time when they become especially vulnerable to heart disease, namely, after fifty years of age."

Embezzled Bone

𝒯he second major thief of menopause is osteoporosis. In one third of women, bad cells (osteoclasts) literally cut up the lacelike web of bone matter faster than the good cells (osteoblasts) can rebuild those webs. One doesn't feel a thing. The very stealthiness of this disease is its major threat.

Margie is very good at giving care to everyone else—her laundry-toting postadolescent kids and the battered women she works with at the community center in her college town. Still blond, though aware she is white at the roots, Margie will turn fifty this year. "Oh, shit, my number's up" was her reaction. Her doctor told her ten years ago she was a sitting duck for osteoporosis. Small-boned, she remembers her statuesque mother shrinking about seven inches to a mere five feet tall before she died. "I already know I have bone thinning," she admits.

Typically she resists addressing the issue because that would mean her good-bye to youth. "I'll take hormones when I get there."

"What's *there*?" her girlfriend challenged her.

"You know, old."

Old is too old to start protecting bones. By the time anybody can see osteoporosis, it's too late to reverse it. As you'll recall, we begin to lose bone after the age of thirty-five; the normal rate of loss is about one percent a year. "When you hit fifty, bone loss accelerates to about a percent and a half each year for about ten years," says epidemiologist Trudy Bush, quoting the studies. "Then it levels off again at one percent a year."

Two factors determine a woman's risk of having significant bone loss during this transition. First, her genetic background, and here nature turns the tables on our Western beauty ideal. "I could look at a woman and bet her risks of osteoporosis—fair-skinned, very thin, a smoker, and an early menopause—and usually she'll be symptomatic," says Dr. Lewis Kuller of the University of Pittsburgh School of Public Health.

The second factor is: How strong are the bones a woman has built at her peak? About one third of American women of all ages are calcium-deficient. "The preoccupation of teenage girls is with thin thighs, not good bone, so they get into the habit of drinking diet soda instead of milk," laments Dr. Barrett-Connor. But generational differences here are striking. The frail women who are now immobilized in nursing homes are a different breed from baby boomers who are out there bouncing from work to gym in their nitrogen-cushioned aerobic shoes, popping calcium and snacking on veggies.

Porous bones, which lead to increased risk of fractures, are a major public health problem. One third to one half of all postmenopausal women—and nearly half of all people over age seventy-five—will be affected by this disease, maintains the National Osteoporosis Foundation. Almost a third of women aged sixty-five and over will suffer spinal fractures. And of those who fall and fracture a hip, one in five will not survive a year (usually because of postsurgical complications).

Untreated, not only do older women die from the consequences of osteoporosis, but it often leaves older women frail, susceptible to falls and broken bones, as well as to the little tortures of hairline fractures in the bones they use for walking and bending—and this by their sixties. Later, in their seventies, osteoporosis makes it painful merely to sit on hipbones pulverized almost into powder; it keeps many women homebound, later even chairbound, and is one of the primary reasons an independent woman will finally succumb to nursing home admission.

Taking calcium supplements *alone* cannot undo the damage done by the loss of estrogen during the period of accelerated loss. And contrary to conventional wisdom, exercise *by itself* is also ineffective in preventing bone loss. These were the results of a study on prevention of postmenopausal osteoporosis reported in the *New England Journal of Medicine* (October 24, 1991). Two regimens were found to be effective. An exercise program *plus* calcium supplements slowed or stopped bone loss. The best results were obtained when estrogen was combined with exercise: Bone mass was *increased*, and other symptoms—hot flashes and sleeplessness—improved after three months.

Vitamin K has been found to inhibit the precipitous loss of calcium in postmenopausal women by up to 50 percent, in a study from the Netherlands. Dark green leafy vegetables like broccoli and brussels sprouts are sources of Vitamin K.

What kind of exercise works for osteoporosis prevention? The slogging pedaler on a stationary bike is not doing her bones much good, and swimming doesn't help, according to Dr. Richard Bockman, head of the endocrinology department and codirector of the Osteoporosis Center at New York's Hospital for Special Surgery. The weight of the body has to be carried by the bones in order to stimulate bone strength. Brisk jogging requires a push-off that is much greater than one's body weight. The point is that one *needs stress* on that hip, and brisk walking can increase that stress in a natural way. "Everyone can walk briskly," encourages Dr. Bockman. "Or do serious walking on a treadmill at a tilt, which gives you both weight-bearing and aerobic benefit."

Robert Lindsay's study group at the Helen Hayes Bone Center confirms a measurable prevention of bone loss in postmenopausal women treated with 0.625 mg of Premarin plus Provera. It is not uncommon today to see women started on estrogen at age sixty or older. It is not too late. "There is pretty good evidence that giving estrogen will slow any further bone loss at least up until the age of seventy-five," says Dr. Lindsay. Estrogen won't reverse the attrition that has already taken place, but it will stop it from getting worse, he adds.

Dr. Stanley Birge at Washington University has introduced a radical notion into the debate: "The effect of estrogen on protecting against bone fractures may be due to maintaining high mental functioning." In the OASIS Fall and Hip Fracture Study, women over seventy who were on estrogen performed better on tasks measuring mental processing speed than women of the same age and education who were not on the hormone. Dr. Birge postulates that estrogen-deprived women over seventy are more likely to suffer the dreaded hip fracture, because when they lose their balance, they don't respond fast enough to break their fall. "Whereas women of the same age who had wrist fractures—evidence they did respond and break their fall—showed twice the mental processing speed."

Technological advances in machinery now make it possible to measure precisely the weight and strength of a woman's bones. Most major American cities with a medical center or university have bone densitometer machines (although many are used only for research). Whatever regimen of calcium and exercise and/or hormones a woman tries can be evaluated against her own baseline, to show annually how much bone she is maintaining or losing. It's the same principle as having annual mammograms.

"Physicians have to get used to thinking of bone mass measurement just as they think about a blood pressure measurement," urges Dr. Lindsay. Some Blue Cross health plans will pick up part of the cost of osteoporosis testing. Medicare does not yet reimburse for bone mass measurement. With regard to bone disease in older women, we are exactly where we were with breast cancer twenty years ago: Osteoporosis prevention hasn't yet been considered worthy —another example of the scandalous politics of women's health.

Has Anyone Seen My Memory?

~

At forty you can't read the numbers in the telephone book. At fifty you can't remember them. What's going on?

An even more insidious thief is being quietly noted both by pure-science researchers and by doctors who increasingly hear complaints like those of the very smart best-selling author in Colorado whom I happened to phone one day. "How are you?" I asked.

"I'm thinking slower—are you? I have tremendous trouble concentrating. I start to write and just wander. Am I getting stupid?"

All writers have days like this. But this woman, just past fifty, was usually so witty about life's pitfalls. "What I feel is panic," she said. "I tape every interview now, because I know I won't remember. And I'm so intent on remembering, I become extremely irritable. Because if somebody interrupts me while I'm trying to remember, then I'm frightened of losing it."

She wasn't kidding. "You feel less competitive, slow off the mark," she went on. "I think the bottom line is," she said glumly, "I'm just plain dimmer."

Wait a minute, hadn't she been all smiles after having had a hysterectomy three years earlier? "Oh, sure, I was just so glad to be finished with cysts and fibroids, and I was mad at all these doctors." The surgeon told her they had saved one ovary, which should produce enough estrogen; she wouldn't need to take hormones. That was three years before.

"You might be suffering from estrogen deprivation," I said.

"You mean, I'm not stupid, I just need hormones?"

I told her story to Barbara Sherwin, the McGill University professor. After the age of forty-eight, she said, that remaining ovary would be quickly withering away. Moreover, manipulation during surgery to remove the uterus often compromises the blood supply to the ovaries. Professor Sherwin said she would be shocked if the writer's estrogen level weren't in the postmenopausal range. And the impact on mental acuity can be quite noticeable.

"Something has happened to my memory," the working women who walk into McGill University Menopause Clinic will often report. They misplace things. It's harder to remember a new phone number, though they always remember the old ones. "People start getting methodical. They don't just put their glasses down on the kitchen counter; they put them down in a specific spot," notes Professor Sherwin. Though this temporary strain on short-term memory is quantifiable, the women are not seriously impaired in their daily functioning.

The few studies showing that estrogen loss has a deleterious effect on mental functioning have been done on surgically menopausal women, where the hormonal drop is sudden and acute. For naturally menopausal women, the effect may be a little fuzzy thinking in the early years of Change of Life. "When I was in my early fifties, it was impossible for me to look something up in an index and hold three different page numbers in my head," chuckles

Canadian newsletter editor O'Leary Cobb. "I'm fifty-seven now, and it's all come back again. Most of us do recover."

Estrogen does help increase the blood flow to the brain. Some women say their memory becomes more acute than ever after they start taking estrogen. The absence of estrogen has a powerful effect on synapses at certain sites in the brain, confirms Dr. Bruce McEwen, a neuroendocrinologist at Rockefeller University. He has observed brain chemistry changes in rats during the equivalent of menopause (after their ovaries were removed). "The number of synaptic connections actually decreases. If you administer estrogens, these synaptic connections are remade within a few days." During the female rat's four-day estrous cycle, which mimics the menstrual cycle, these synapses come and go. As for human females, it has been demonstrated that estrogens do have an effect on mental functioning—not on IQ but in terms of performance—though Dr. McEwen is quick to point out our state of scientific ignorance. "No one has bothered to look at cognitive behavior and the effect of estrogen therapy in a long-term study." He emphasizes that the subjective experience of cloudy thinking at times during menopause can be equated, for instance, to jet lag: "It's mostly transient and certainly reversible."

Sure enough, when my writer friend from Colorado went to a gynecologist for her first pelvic exam in four years, the doctor said, "Your vaginal walls are bone-dry." It was immediately obvious from her age that she needed estrogen. "I feel infinitely better, more alert, more moist, more like my old self," she said. Having overcome her initial resistance to HRT, she now believes she will likely live a longer, healthier life. "You get on a track—with regular reminders to get mammograms and Pap smears. If something does go wrong, you have an early warning system set up to catch it."

There is mounting evidence that estrogen has a critical impact on the activity of the human brain—in both women and men—throughout the life cycle. Although this is an underexplored area, it is now possible to report that estrogen has a definite effect on cognitive functioning, according to Dr. Sherwin. She has been doing studies over a period of nearly ten years on a total of several hundred women in all stages of life. They are given standardized neuropsychological tests when they are in an estrogenized state and when they are in an estrogen-deprived state. The results are clear, says Dr. Sherwin. "Estrogen helps maintain verbal memory and it enhances a woman's capacity for new learning."

Estrogen also spurs the production of an important enzyme in the brain that helps the connections between brain cells to flourish, making it quicker and easier for messages to leap from one neuron to the next. The inside of a robust, estrogenized brain might look more like the dense telephone wiring in an urban telephone terminal box, while the brain of an older, estrogen-deprived woman or man might look more like the sparse wiring of a rural telephone substation.

The results are most dramatic in healthy, functioning women who are tested just before they have a hysterectomy where their ovaries are removed. After the operation, their scores on tests of verbal memory and retention of new material decrease significantly. But Dr. Sherwin is quick to point out that they could still perform reasonably in their jobs and manage their lives. However, those who were given estrogen therapy postoperatively performed comparatively better. All the women she has tested decided to take hormone replacement once the trials were completed.

Estrogen has recently been posited as a woman's best defense against organic brain disease in later life. In a study of 2,418 women by Dr. Victor Henderson of the University of Southern California, those on hormone replacement were much less likely to develop Alzheimer's disease than women who had never taken hormones.

Dangerous Breasts

$\mathcal{O}$nly four years ago the number of American women diagnosed with breast cancer was one in ten; now it is one in nine. The breast cancer phobia has now overtaken almost all other health issues surrounding menopause for many American women, particularly those who have had a brush with it anywhere in their family. As to why we focus more on women with breast cancer than on those with heart disease, Dr. Trudy Bush notes that although two thirds of all breast cancers are postmenopausal, one third do occur in younger women, "so you're thinking of the tragic cases among women forty to fifty-two."

A woman I'll call Sarah was brutally widowed in her prime of a dashing, beloved, prominent husband. She was left with a lovely apartment and a terrace garden she let go to seed because she couldn't bear for several years to step out on it and be assaulted by painful memories evoked by the sun and beauty. Sarah was a freelance commercial artist, and a very successful one. But in her misery she soon became blocked creatively and desperately lonely.

Then to top it off—hot flashes. Hearing about "vaginal

dryness" from her friends, she wondered if she would lose interest in sex before she had it again. The whole terror of being identified as a menopausal woman overtook her. "And I'm single, so it matters."

Off to the plastic surgeon for a full face-and-neck-lift. Then to the gynecologist for something to "take away the embarrassment of these drippy hot flashes at dinner parties." She had to keep herself shelf-fresh—not like some postdated yogurt—if she was going to keep hope alive for recovering her creativity and her zest for finding a new partner in life.

"But I have these dangerous breasts," she told me, stroking the unusually large, well-formed bosoms under her T-shirt, as if they had grown alien and were ready at any point to turn on her. "I have a history of breast cancer among the women in my family." So, before giving herself hormones, she consulted two other doctors, one a reproductive oncologist. Both said, "Take the hormones. It's worth the benefit."

"But I admit I did it—do it—with great trepidation. Are you on them? Why? Why don't you get off?" The feverish questioning revealed her frustration and suppressed fears. I talked about my primary concern being prevention of osteoporosis and heart disease—the major dangers for older women. Like most of my most educated and savvy friends, she didn't know heart disease was the number one killer.

"I also have osteoporosis in my family," she said miserably. "So what do I do? I've been on for five years. My doctor never mentioned any end point."

Doctors seldom do, I said.

"All I know is that once I started taking hormones, the flashes stopped and I had a feeling of well-being. And I looked okay. All that is important to me because I'm an older single woman. So my philosophy has been, If it's working, don't mess with it. But am I doing something to my body that I'll kick myself for later?"

She had had a bone density test a couple years before and was told she was fine; the hormones were working. Now she has a new male partner, and she's brought her terrace garden back to life. It's a place of delight where we sat that June day, surrounded by sprouting shrubs and exquisite coral roses, birdsong, and cool breeze. "It gives me such a lift when I wake up to come out here," Sarah said. She's become a happy, healthy, fully functioning, attractive and sexual woman again. Hormones appear to be integral to her quality of life in her mid-fifties. What risk is she running by taking HRT?

Dr. Hiram Cody, the New York Hospital breast surgeon, stresses: "When you're doing a family history, keep in mind that only a first-degree relative—mother or sister—poses an added risk. If it's a grandmother, aunt, or cousin, it's not nearly the same added risk, if any risk at all." Also, to be relevant, one's mother had to have been under the age of fifty when she developed the breast cancer. "It's a premenopausal first-degree relative who contributes a significantly increased risk of breast cancer," affirms the leading researcher on menopause in Britain, Dr. Malcolm Whitehead. "Even with the worst possible family history," adds Dr. Cody, "a woman has no more than a fifty-fifty chance of getting breast cancer."

Studies that attempt to document any causative link between HRT and breast cancer are doomed to be inconclusive because the usual dose of Premarin provides only one quarter of the estrogen that a woman's fertile ovaries would produce. But it can be said that the more cycles a woman has, naturally and synthetically, the more estrogen she has in her system over a lifetime.

The primates researcher Kim Wallen points out that for thousands of years most women cycled only two or three times before becoming pregnant, followed by several years of nursing, which again suppressed their periods; then they cycled again several times before the next pregnancies. Historically, then, a woman in her reproductive years may have had a total of forty or fifty ovarian cycles. The modern woman may have more than three hundred. "So human females today are getting a very different pattern of hormonal stimulation," he concludes. "Then, when they go through menopause, we are hitting them with another period of exposure to hormones that they never would have had in the past."

The general world medical consensus from the best studies is that no evidence suggests there is any danger of increasing the risk of breast cancer by taking HRT for up to five or six years. Quite a number of studies report no danger for possibly up to ten years.

The PEPI trial, completed in 1994, found no hint of an increase in breast cancer in women being given hormone replacement therapy. It was only a three-year study, however, not long enough to make any claims. Dr. Elizabeth L. Barrett-Connor, a principal investigator, is cautiously optimistic. "I think estrogen is safe for five to seven years," she says. "After that, I don't know." Menopausal women are already instinctively following roughly the same yardstick: The average length of time that women continue on HRT is 4.6 years.

The risk of breast cancer does increase after ten years on HRT, but just how much has not been reliably determined; it ranges from 10 to 25 percent. But although there is an increase in *diagnosis* of breast cancer after ten years in women on HRT, there is no increase in *death rates* from breast cancer, as compared to women who have never used hormones. In fact, studies of middle-class American women who take HRT indicate they live longer—with a 20 to 40 percent reduction in mortality rate from any and all causes.

So why do women back off?

"Women are very well aware of the one in nine statistic

for breast cancer," says Dr. Trudy Bush. "We have to teach them that it's a six in nine risk for getting cardiovascular disease."

It is a well-established fact by now that heart disease kills four times as many women as breast cancer does. There are, however, women whose family history or lifestyle puts them at much higher risk for breast cancer. Overall, it appears that the risk of breast cancer from using hormones is highest for women who tend to have excessive levels of estrogen already. An overweight woman with lots of fat cells has a built-in risk factor. Other risk factors (in addition to the genetic predisposition that can now be detected) are early menarche, first pregnancy at a late age, or no children, all of which add to the lifetime levels of estrogen. Dietary risk factors include a habit of more than seven alcoholic drinks a week, possibly low levels of Vitamin A from a diet poor in green leafy vegetables and beta-carotene, and high fat intake. International health statistics point to a much higher incidence of breast cancer in countries where women eat a high-fat diet.

Also, as a generation, boomer women carry an increased estrogen load, having been the first to use both oral contraceptives and estrogen therapy. If you are still premenopausal, I would urge to you consider your lifetime "estrogen budget"—counting your periods from how early you entered menarche, adding the number of years you may have taken birth control pills, the high doses of estrogen you may have added if you ever took fertility drugs, and subtracting for the number of pregnancies you have supported.

Another expert emphasizes high fat diets as the chief culprit in increasing breast cancer rates among American women. Dr. Caldwell Esselstyn, Jr., is a maverick surgeon who campaigns for health care "beyond surgery." As president of the American Association of Endocrine Surgeons, Dr. Esselstyn starts with the data that show nations that consume greater amounts of fat per person have the highest mortality rates of breast cancer. "And we know that rural Japanese women who still eat a low-fat diet of vegetables, rice, and a little fish experience far less breast cancer than Japanese women who have become urbanized and now like steak and french fries," he says. "If the lobules and ducts of the breast are constantly being overstimulated by a high fat intake, which leads to higher production of estrogen, it stands to reason they will be more likely to have cell changes leading to cancer."

Not only does a fatty diet add indirectly to the risk of breast cancer by increasing the estrogen level, but most recently basic scientists have demonstrated in the laboratory that fat also has a direct effect on tumor growth *independent of estrogen*. Dr. David Rose at the American Health Foundation in Valhalla, New York, injected human female breast cancer cells into two groups of mice. He gave one group a diet of 23 percent corn oil, the same type of fat found in popular margarines. This high-fat diet both increased and accelerated the growth and spread of tumors as compared with the low-fat group. Rose's results, published in the *Journal of the National Cancer Institute* (October 1991), provide a compelling argument against high-fat diets to protect a woman from *both* heart disease and breast cancer.

"Nobody is arguing against estrogen supplement for the short term—the first three to five years of perimenopause and menopause," says Dr. Kuller, the public health expert at the University of Pittsburgh. "But for the long term, meaning ten to fifteen years, estrogen is drug therapy and should only be prescribed for women predisposed to osteoporosis or heart disease, or both." Dr. Kathi Hanna, senior analyst for the Office of Technology Assessment, a research arm of Congress that has surveyed existing studies, agrees: "It's alarming that practitioners are talking about using hormone therapy indefinitely."

But here's the rub. The key to hormonal protection

against heart disease in older women, according to the Nurses' Health Study, was that the healthy women were taking estrogen currently. The risks and benefits of estrogen therapy on eight separate health conditions were toted up in a thorough review by T. M. Mack at the University of Southern California. Stopping treatment with estrogen at the end of five years would produce a moderate reduction in the expected hospitalizations for breast cancer. But it would also virtually eliminate all the benefits of long-term health enhancement—a discomfiting choice!

But at least we have choices.

The Weight-Gain Fallacy

~

𝒜mong those women who are given prescriptions for HRT, fully half of them either don't take the hormones as prescribed or throw out their pills within less than a year. Why? According to my medical colleagues on the advisory board to the Women's Health Initiative, the two main reasons women resist or discontinue taking hormones are fear of breast cancer and weight gain.

Women invariably blame hormones for whatever weight gain occurs over the next few years once they start taking HRT. The number one side effect named in a survey by *Prevention* magazine was weight gain, reported by 60 percent of women who took hormones.* What most of us don't understand (or don't want to accept) is that a dramatic change in metabolism takes place in both women and men in middle life. In women that change coincidentally corresponds with the menopause transition, which usually gets blamed for it.

---

*Cathy Perlmutter, Toby Hanlon and Maureen Sangiorgio, "Triumph Over Menopause," *Prevention*, August 1994, pp. 78–87, 137, 142.

"Women preserve their fat-free mass quite well, relatively speaking, up to about age forty-eight or forty-nine, with little age effect," according to Eric Poehlman, Ph.D., associate professor of gerontology at Veterans Administration Medical Center in Baltimore, who has studied hormonal changes related to food, diet, and exercise in many different populations. "But there's a significant change after age forty-nine, about a 4 or 5 percent decline in fat-free body mass. And that is in healthy women *not* on HRT."

The PEPI study confirmed this conclusion. The women who gained the most weight during the three-year trial were those who took no hormone therapy at all. And over large studies it has been found that women who take estrogen tend to weigh less and be thinner than women who do not.

The good news is that a woman can wipe out the age effect on her weight—with exercise. Resistance training (with weights), if started before she enters menopause, can prevent or at least blunt the age-related decline in her resting metabolic rate, says Poehlman.

On balance, hormone replacement looks like a good way for most women to support a longer, healthier life. But so does exercise and diet modification—eating lightly with low fat foods, exercising an hour a day at least four times a week, and using soybean products (which are high in natural estrogen).

The PEPI Study Breakthrough

$\mathscr{B}$elieve it or not, when I first published this book, in 1992, no study had been completed in North America on the possible carcinogenic consequences of the combined hormone therapy routinely prescribed for women in menopause. Can you imagine millions of men over fifty—those at the highest levels of the power structure—being herded by doctors toward chemical dependence on powerful hormones suspected of causing testicular cancer? We are a generation of hormone guinea pigs.

But happily in the last few years, women in multiple disciplines have begun to use their awareness and power to change the course of women's health.

In the early Nineties a group of baby-boom-age women in scientific research campaigned to get government and private funding to launch the first preliminary study on the effects of hormone replacement therapy—the Postmenopausal Estrogen/Progestin Intervention—or PEPI, as it is known. It was a three-year study of 875 women that tried out various drugs in different combinations. The results, published in early 1995, will help women and their doctors to customize the management of menopause. The most welcome finding was a strong confirmation that estrogen, taken alone or taken with progesterone, cuts the potential of heart disease among women in half. It also reduces by 50 percent their risk of dying from a heart attack. The addition of progesterone did not negate the benefits of estrogen, as had been suspected for many years.

Further, the study addressed a long-standing problem women have with HRT. The standard treatment has been 10 mg of Provera, a synthetic progesterone, to be taken for ten days along with Premarin (estrogen). The well-being promoted by the estrogen, however, is frequently overshadowed by sensations of bloating, crampiness, irritability, brought on when the Provera is introduced. Women taking the Provera who are startled by feeling unpleasantly premenstrual and having their periods start up all over again often call their doctors and say, "Why did you give me that stuff?"

But in order to protect against uterine cancer, most physicians continued to insist their patients take large doses of Provera along with their estrogen. When women are given no other choice than this combination, they often bag the whole idea of hormone replacement or, more dangerously, simply drop the protective progesterone. Osteoporosis experts, such as Dr. Robert Lindsay at the Helen Hayes Bone Center, fret that "many people who would gain in healthy active years on estrogen replacement are turned off by the required addition of a progestin and the continuation of periods."

The welcome news is the PEPI study found a woman doesn't need the "elephant gun" dose of progesterone that had been routinely prescribed. Instead, a much smaller dose of a progesterone (2.5 mg), taken every day along with the estrogen, protected the uterus. And for the first time a scientific study gave a blessing to other alternatives, including a natural form of progesterone.

Women constantly ask me at lectures, "How come so

many women in Europe use natural hormones?" I've often asked people in the American medical establishment the same thing. "We just don't believe in medicating with plants and barks," is the usual contemptuous reply. "Who knows what dangerous effects they might have or what dose to use?" The American medical-pharmaceutical establishment persists in fostering suspicion of any "natural" compound that might alleviate symptoms—a shaky position given the many plants and barks from which major drugs such as digitalis and even aspirin are derived.

Fortunately, the women who designed the PEPI trial did not share this outmoded bias. In addition to testing the synthetic hormone products on the market, they pushed to include a natural compound meant to protect the uterus against cancer. It is called natural micronized progesterone. Made from Mexican yams or soybeans, natural progesterone matches closely the chemical composition of the body's own progesterone. It is therefore less likely to confuse the body and lead to salt buildup, fluid retention, and hypoglycemia. *Micronized* means that the particles are finely ground and thus are more completely absorbed.

In the first edition of *The Silent Passage*, I reported that new-generation gynecologists and research scientists, such as Dr. Jamie Grifo at New York Hospital–Cornell Medical Center, believed natural micronized progesterone to be the wave of the future. But American physicians have been reluctant to prescribe it because it doesn't have FDA approval. "What's the problem?" I remember asking Dr. Grifo in 1992. "Why aren't women being given more choices?"

As a frustrated clinician and researcher, Dr. Grifo was candid. "The bottom line is, the right studies need to be done for the right length of time, and clearly, for economic and political reasons, they're not. Why? Who supports the majority of the research? The drug companies."

"We were going out on a limb [to test natural progesterone], but I'm glad we did," confided University of Maryland epidemiologist Trudy Bush, Ph.D., who, along with Dr. Elizabeth L. Barrett-Connor, was one of the principal investigators for PEPI. Their boldness paid off in good news. A continuous dose of the natural micronized progesterone in combination with estrogen every day turned out to be the best combination of hormones for women with a uterus. That regimen produced the best overall cardiovascular effect and also proved to protect a woman against the risk of uterine cancer. And, most important to patients, the natural progesterone presented fewer unpleasant side effects compared with the synthetic version.

This is the first time that an NIH-funded scientific investigation into hormone therapy has given credibility to a natural compound. Dr. Joel Hargrove, an obstetrician-gynecologist in private practice and a well-respected research scientist at Vanderbilt University Hospital in Nashville, Tennesee, has done a number of smaller studies on natural progesterone. He used to use 200–300 mg but since has discovered that such a large dose is unnecessary. He finds that 100 mg per day prevents any unnatural growth of the lining of the uterus in most women. The body produces progesterone by pulsations about every twenty minutes, so it isn't as beneficial to take it just once a day. Wally Simons, pharmacist at the popular mail-order International Women's Pharmacy in Madison, Wisconsin, suggests that it is better for the balance of one's system to take 50 or 100 mg of natural progesterone twice a day.

Progesterone is a calming hormone. Simons reports anecdotally that women find natural progesterone sometimes has an anti-anxiety effect. It is also a natural diuretic, so it can alleviate the water retention produced by estrogen. The natural micronized progesterone used in the PEPI trial is in an oil base, inside a capsule, which allows it to be picked up by the lymphatic system. Progesterone, whether taken by capsule or tablet, can aggravate candida, a systemic yeast infection. If a woman has that problem, she can cut open an oil-based capsule of natural progesterone and rub it anywhere on her skin, allowing it to be absorbed transdermally rather than through her digestive system.

There is only one problem with this good news. American women can't easily get natural micronized progesterone, because it has not been approved by the FDA.

Schering-Plough, the German company that supplied it to the PEPI trial for experimentation, sells the product in Europe but had not applied for FDA approval and thus could not sell it in the U.S. The only way a woman can get hold of this promising compound is if she knows the names and numbers of the few pharmacies in the United States that sell it, and can persuade her doctor to write a prescription for it.*

Intelligent and influential women reacted with anger and disbelief to this Catch-22. Why should women and doctors have to use an underground network to obtain a natural product when a government study, supported by their tax dollars, suggests it may be the safest and most effective choice for combined hormone therapy?

Dr. Bush and I were baffled. She suggested I call the FDA. At first I ran into a wall of bureaucratese. I was told the agency had no applications from any drug company asking to test natural micronized progesterone; end of story. I turned to another of my research partners, Dr. Patricia Allen, who knew the top woman at the FDA, Ruth Merkatz.

---

*The Women's International Pharmacy (800–279–5708) or the Madison Pharmacy (800–558–7046), both in Madison, Wisconsin, are U.S. outlets for oral micronized progesterone (OMP), produced by Upjohn. It is also available through College Pharmacy in Colorado Springs, Colorado (800–888–9358) or Bajamar Women's Health Care in St. Louis, MO (800–255–8025). Wally Simons, the pharmacist at the Women's International, says that synthetic progesterone is from ten to a hundred times as potent as the natural micronized product. As the equivalent of 2.5 mg of Provera, he recommends from 100 to 200 mg a day of natural progesterone, preferably taken half in the morning and half in the evening.

Nurse Merkatz heads the new Office of Women's Health at the drug regulatory agency, a position that didn't even exist a few years ago. Her job is to make sure the FDA is proactive in bringing products to market that will promote women's health.

I asked Ruth Merkatz, If this natural preparation has all the positive benefits one looks for from a progesterone and few of the negative side effects of Provera, why doesn't it have the FDA seal of approval? She promised to get back to me. And ten days later she did. But a lot had transpired in those ten days.

"Big drug companies have been encouraged to submit applications to us for testing natural micronized progesterone," she reported, "and we will accelerate the process." She then brought to the phone Dr. Sol Sobel, head of the FDA's Division of Endocrine and Metabolic Products. He was cautious. "I will grant there is reason to believe that natural micronized progesterone will have a better effect on the lipids [meaning that it increases the protection against heart disease]. But it may be at the cost of less protection of the endometrium [lining of the uterus]."

But even Dr. Sobel had caught the atmosphere of activism. The agency had actually gone out to solicit applications from several drug companies and offered them financial incentives to run clinical trials on the product. "It's quite possible," Dr. Sobel ventured, "if proper doses of micronized progesterone are presented to us, we may be able to establish the lowest effective dose to protect the endometrium and get that drug on the market—in a year or so."

In an agency where a drug can be in clinical trials for seven years at a cost of $150 million dollars just to get the FDA's blessing, this amounts to moving at the speed of light. Such a story would have been inconceivable as little as five years ago.

Should I or Shouldn't I?

This is the question that dominates most discussions about menopause among most women, yet there is little agreement. A few basic points need to be made at the outset.

∼ Taking estrogen to replace what her body made is not for every woman. But it *is* for every woman to consider.

∼ If you decide to use hormone therapy, you should do so for a good reason, not just because your doctor hands you a prescription. Many women say they are uneasy about taking drugs for something that is natural, not a disease.

∼ It is also not "natural" to live much beyond menopause. Most of our great-grandmothers did not live long enough to deal with the debilitating consequences of bone loss or heart disease. Exploring HRT as an option is a good way to get yourself thinking about how to protect and enhance your health for the next thirty or forty years.

∼ You don't have to make a decision for life. You make a decision that addresses the phase of menopause you're in right now. When you review it again next season, predictably, you will need custom-tailoring as routinely as you let your skirts up or down, or in or out. If you do decide to try HRT, expect the first year to be trial-and-error. It's important to choose a doctor who recognizes the need to readjust the dose and regimen until your body responds optimally.

Women have a right to good, unbiased information about hormone replacement therapy. HRT is a health issue. Most women who take it do not do so to stay youthful and sexy looking. They take it because they are convinced it is good for their health and mental well-being. They are likely to live longer, more vital lives and to continue to enjoy their sexuality.

Dr. Nita Nelson, a Los Angeles gynecologist, makes the case that estrogen is the only hormone that people are asked to live without. "If a woman is diabetic and doesn't have enough insulin, we don't say, 'Try to live without the insulin.' We know she's going to die sooner and that the years she has left will be poor unless we replace the insulin she's missing. The same goes for thyroid deficiencies. Estrogen is the only one we ask women to do without."

So persuasive is the evidence of the multiple protective benefits of estrogen, a stunning 75 to 95 percent of American obstetrician-gynecologists say they would prescribe hormones to most of their recently menopausal patients. I asked one of the major researchers in Europe, Dr. Malcolm Whitehead, director of the Menopause Clinic at Kings College Hospital in London and president of the International Menopause Society, "If it were your wife, what would you tell her about coming to a decision?

"I don't see it as much of a conundrum, perhaps because I'm a man," he opines. "If estrogens really do reduce coronary-artery disease death by fifty percent, that factor alone will swamp any other factor in the equation." Dr. Whitehead openly envies women for having a choice; men don't. "We are stuck from the time we're born to the time we die with arterial disease as a sword of Damocles hanging over us."

The object for the HRT user is to get as much benefit as possible without adding measurably to her risks. That probably is achieved through moderation: by making a compromise between the maximum state of well-being now—which usually requires high doses of estrogen and progesterone to make a woman feel just as she did before menopause—and the maximum protection of her body for the next three or four decades of life.

There are now at least a dozen different regimens recommended by doctors for combining estrogen and a progesterone. No two women respond the same way. "I always tell people the first year is trial and error," says Barbara Sherwin at the McGill University clinic. "We're constantly readjusting the dose, the types of products, and the regimen."

One new variation in regimen, which the PEPI trial found to be quite effective, has become popular: continuous, low-dose progesterone. Not only does it minimize the nasty side effects for many women, it also eliminates the return of periods, which is the main objection women have to remaining on hormones. A small amount of the progesterone is taken continuously, everyday along with the estrogen. (Some doctors suggest discontinuing both for the last five days of the month.) It usually smoothes out a woman's cycle, she doesn't have storms of hormonal highs and lows, and after six months at most, periods generally cease.

Results of the PEPI study suggest a woman is in almost no danger of uterine cancer if she takes combination therapy: estrogen together with a natural progesterone or a synthetic progestin. But using estrogen alone is hazardous for a woman with a uterus. A surprisingly large number of the subjects given only estrogen had to be taken off this regimen because of precancerous changes in the lining of the uterus. But Dr. Bush passed on relieving news for women who have been taking estrogen alone (often against doctor's advice). Two months after progesterone was introduced to the regimen of those in the trial with precancerous changes, the lining of the uterus returned to normal.

Uterine cancer is a somewhat overrated concern, according to clinicians advising the Women's Health Initiative. Even women taking estrogen who do get endometrial cancer, and have appropriate treatment, live longer than women who never took estrogen and never had uterine cancer—a startling statistic. Nevertheless, using combined hormone therapy can diminish the chance of uterine cancer from the start.

Periodic ultrasound exams have become an additional way for a woman to monitor both the health of her uterine lining and her ovaries. (Unlike mammograms, however, pelvic sonograms are not covered by most health insurance plans as preventive medicine.) If any major thickening or unevenness of the lining is seen on ultrasound, a relatively painless endometrial biopsy or a D&C can be done. Abnormal bleeding patterns may also be an early warning of precancerous changes in the lining of the uterus. However, this early sign does not always occur, warns Dr. Allen. Fortunately, the uterine lining is not difficult to monitor. A D&C can be easily performed and a woman can be taken off hormones for a while until her uterus settles down. There is a high cure rate with uterine cancer that is caught early.

The Estraderm patch is an increasingly popular method of delivering estrogen to the body. A small adhesive bandage releases the hormone through the skin, with the advantage that it maintains a continuous, consistent level of estrogen in the system, like a time-release capsule. It is not metabolized through the liver and therefore has no impact on digestive diseases such as ulcers. The FDA has approved Estraderm as a treatment for menopause and osteoporosis. Estrogen delivered in this form, however, has not proven to be as beneficial in protecting against heart disease as estrogen taken orally.

At least one scientist with long experience in studying women who use hormone replacement therapy has unresolved questions about the transdermal patch. It can easily return a woman to a premenopausal state. That sounds desirable, and may explain why women are so enthusiastic about the patch, but there is another side to the story. According to studies done by Dr. Brian Henderson, the patch produces higher levels of the most potent form of estrogen (estradiol) than does Premarin, giving a woman almost as much hormone as she would have made herself. "The effect of that should be to make one's breast cancer risk go up substantially more on the patch than on Premarin," says Dr. Henderson. He points out that Premarin has been used for fifty years, while the patch has been widely available for only the last seven years.

The situation for victims of breast cancer is that they often are doubly deprived. Until recently, it has been considered verboten to give hormone replacement therapy to a postmenopausal woman with breast cancer. Today, for women with a terribly symptomatic menopause adding to their depression over losing a breast, the quality of life issue must be weighed in the balance. Especially if they have had a hysterectomy and have no circulating hormones at all, they may feel life is hardly worth living. Some physicians now offer them the choice of taking a short course of HRT.

The FDA has finally recognized the need for a study of this issue. Dr. Avrum Bluming, a clinical professor of medicine at USC, believes that data already suggest a greater benefit than risk in taking HRT for women with a history of successfully treated breast cancer. But no definitive conclusions will be available until he has followed up on his pilot study of 150 patients for at least three years.

Much more hopeful is the drug tamoxifen. There is considerable evidence by now that tamoxifen may offer the benefits of hormone replacement therapy for the heart and bones of a woman who has had breast cancer, while also reducing her risk of a recurrence.

If you have had a precancerous condition in the cervix, not to worry; cervical cancer is not hormone dependent. Also, there is no evidence that estrogen increases the risk of ovarian cancer.

The debate over "natural" vs. "medicalized" menopause will only grow more vigorous as boomers come along. I was asked to give a talk in San Diego to women state legislators from all over the country on the subject of menopause. It was quite amazing: Four hundred busy political women stayed for several hours on the last Sunday of their conference to discuss every aspect of the Change. Many of them came to microphones to describe their experiences. One lawmaker from Minnesota told how a group of her peers in the state capital decided they weren't going to skulk around and hide their postmenopausal status—they were going to flaunt it. So they formed a bike club and rode to the statehouse wearing Day-Glo pink T-shirts with THE HOT FLASHES printed in black letters across the front. Finally Betty Friedan took her turn and pooh-poohed the whole subject. Hormones were dangerous, and besides, who needs them? Drawing only on her own experience, she shrugged. "I may have had a hot flash, one hot flash, while I was giving a major speech in the middle of the Seventies."

But no one woman's genetic makeup should be held up as the model for abstinence from hormones, making the next woman feel lesser for having a different nervous system, different metabolism, and different stores of hormones, just as she has different depths of pigment and strands of DNA in the tangle of her own creation.

"We wear glasses when our eyes are bad, we use hearing aids, we get false teeth, and now we're putting in new knees and hips," counters Columbia University physiologist Fredi Kronenberg, a researcher in rehabilitation medicine at Columbia University Hospital of Physicians and Surgeons. "Estrogen affects our hearts, our minds, our bones, our behavior, and our sexual function and desire." Her basic argument is, How can women expect to live thirty-five more years and not supplement the estrogen they no longer make naturally?

Several studies indicate that women live longer if they are on estrogen, notably the Leisure World Study of 8,881 women aged forty through 101 in a Southern California retirement community. The women, all white, upper-middle class, completed a health survey in 1981 and were followed up seven years later. "The women who used Premarin for the longest time had the lowest death rate," says Dr. Brian Henderson, who assembled the cohort. The more startling evidence from the 1991 follow-up is that *current users* who had taken estrogen for more than fifteen years, and were by then in their seventies and eighties, enjoyed *twice the benefit*—a 40 percent reduction—in their overall mortality.

"Women with symptoms certainly feel better when they take estrogen, and those in professional positions almost always feel they work and concentrate better," concludes Dr. Lindsay. The standard comment volunteered by British women who have been on long-term hormone replacement therapy, according to Dr. Whitehead, is: "They say they feel fit, and they always seem to have four times as much energy as their neighbors do."

To make it easy for your doctor to take care of you during these years, know what you want. Here are questions to ask yourself:

∼ Is there any evidence of osteoporosis in your family?

∼ Did your mother or a sister have breast cancer? How young? Was it estrogen-sensitive?

∼ Is there any family history of heart disease?

∼ Is there a family history of cancer of the uterus?

∼ Did you have serious PMS?

∼ How long have you been perimenopausal? (The longer it takes you to move from irregular cycles to no cycles, the more likely you are to have physical and emotional symptoms.)

∼ Rank, on a scale of one to ten, what concerns you most about menopause—i.e., No. 1 might be the embarrassment of hot flashes in public, and No. 10 might be the fear of breast cancer or of losing memory and concentration.

It's natural to want to put off asking ourselves such questions as long as possible, if not forever. But remember the goal that was stated at the outset of this book. You can now plan for your menopause the way you planned for your pregnancies. The best way to begin is to become knowledgeable enough that you have ten pertinent questions to ask about your menopause when the need arises. That's empowerment.

Cost-Benefits of Hormone Replacement Therapy

~

Risks	Benefits
1. Possible increased risk of cancer of uterus	1. Prevents osteoporosis
2. Small increase in risk of breast cancer with prolonged use	2. Decreases heart attacks
3. Continued menstruation or breakthrough bleeding possible	3. No hot flashes
4. Breast swelling or pain	4. Decreases insomnia
5. Premenstrual-like syndrome on some synthetic progesterones	5. Improves energy
6. Expense of doctor visits and screening tests	6. Improves mood and sense of well-being
	7. Restores sexual interest and comfort
	8. Improves concentration and memory
	9. May improve longevity

Commonly Used Hormonal Regimens

Hormone	Method	Common Trade Names
Estrogen	Oral	Estrace Estratab Premarin*
	Skin patch Injection	Estraderm Depo-Estradiol Premarin IV
	Skin cream Vaginal cream	Estrogel Estrace vaginal cream Premarin vaginal cream
Progesterone & Progestins	Oral	Natural Micronized Progesterone Aygestin Cycrin Norlutin Provera
Estrogen/ Progestin Combination	Oral	Premphase (sequential therapy) Prempro (continuous therapy)
Androgens	Oral	Halotestin Oreton Metandren
Estrogen/ Androgen Combination	Oral	Estratest Premarin with methyltestosterone

---

*The two regimens now approved by FDA: (1) Premarin for fifteen days alone, with 10 mg of progesterone added for the last ten days of the month. (2) a daily combination of Premarin and 2.5 mg of Cycrin, which is the same as Provera.

Do I Have to Stay on Hormones Forever?

$\mathcal{O}$ne of the often-repeated scare statements is that hormones will only put off the inevitable. "A woman who starts on hormones will have to stay on forever because if she stops, all the menopausal symptoms will return with a vengeance," a prominent New York gynecologist told a new patient. This "express train" scenario is false, says Dr. Lila A. Wallis, a New York internist with forty years of clinical experience and many older patients who have grown into their sixties under her care as users of hormone replacement therapy.

"In the very early menopause, women require larger doses of estrogens in order to control their symptoms," says Dr. Wallis. "As they get older, the estrogens can be cut down and the patient is more tolerant of the decreased dose."

The one action to avoid is going off hormones "cold turkey." The operative generalization is this: *The more abrupt the drop in estrogen, the more severe are the symptoms.* This explains the severity of symptoms often reported after a hysterectomy or during a sudden, stress-related menopause, just as it explains the flare-up of symptoms that may occur if a woman who's been suppressing them for a decade with HRT abruptly discontinues the hormone bath to which the body is accustomed. There is a simple way to avoid this problem: tapering off. Dr. Wallis advises her older patients to watch the "pause" at the end of the month and note whether or not hot flashes or any other symptoms resurface. As symptoms subside, the regimen of replacement hormones can be gradually reduced. The body is allowed to adjust over time.

Help Is on the Way

~

If we approach this journey with optimism, determined to become informed consumers of health information and choosy about the physician who will work with us as a partner, most of us can live and love and work and cope quite well. Here are three important ways to think about the passage through menopause:

First, consider the time you have left to live—one half your adult life. If you have the good fortune to reach menopause, you have a responsibility to educate yourself on how to preserve your physical and mental well-being so that your older years can be vigorous and independent. Think of going for the long haul. Take a life review of where you have been, the parts of yourself you have already lived out, and those yearnings you left behind as a girl. How can you put play back into your life? How can you turn your talents and life skills to caregiving in the broader, even worldly sphere? What adventure of mind or heart or bold personal challenge would your ideal future self dare to take. Consult her; then follow her lead!

Second, find the information you need to help you manage

your menopausal transition. A woman's wellness center may be sufficient to answer your questions. Most doctors will tell you if you ask them honestly: How many women do you treat over the age of forty-five? (That will tell you how interested or experienced the physician is in treating menopause.) Ask the doctor to describe menopause to you. Then ask questions. If your inquiries are brushed off with pat or curt answers, walk away. There is no clear menopausal test. But if you want some hormonal guidelines, the tests to ask for are your estrogen level, your LH and FSH levels, and an osteoporosis screening. But your best guide is your own symptoms.

Be an inquiring, even challenging partner, not a passive follower of doctor-as-God. Decisions on how to plan for the health and well-being of your next thirty years or more cannot be made in a twenty-minute visit with your doctor, any more than you would decide in twenty minutes on the purchase of a house you may live in for many years. Expect a year of trial and error.

Third, take charge of the transformation. That means becoming serious about regular exercise. Find something you like to do: it's best if it requires making an appointment or a social date because then you'll have to keep to it, but you can also park at the end of the mall and walk briskly with march music on your Walkman. This physical effort will support your bones, heart, lungs, as it pumps oxygen for clear thinking and endorphins for good feeling straight to your brain. Transformation also means looking for ways to stop pushing yourself so hard professionally or inviting so much stress. It may help to find a therapist or a group to work with in identifying the woman you want to be for the rest of your life. Finally, this momentous passage invites meditation and spiritual exploration. A wisewoman will make time to contemplate things eternal and appreciate the life she has.

Coalescence

$\mathcal{O}$nce the ovarian transition is complete, a woman enters a new state of equilibrium. Her energy, moods, and overall sense of physical and mental well-being should be restored, but with a difference. Think of it as discarding the shell of the reproductive self—who came into being in adolescence —and coming out the other side to *coalescence*. (*Coalesce* means "to come together," "to unite"; *escence* denotes "action or process," a change state.)

It is a time when all the wisdom a woman has gathered from fifty years of experience in living comes together. Once she is no longer confined to the culture's definition of woman as a primarily sexual object and breeder, a full unity of her feminine and masculine sides is possible. As she moves beyond gender definition, she gains new license to speak her mind and initiate action.

The time sense changes. People in their late thirties and

early forties are commonly pursued by a frantic hurry-up feeling—as if everything they have missed out on must be seized immediately or lost forever. This midlife agitation is often revived for women by the perimenopausal panic in the mid to late forties. As suggested, the foreshortening of time sense takes place because the forties represent the old age of youth, while the fifties open up the youth of Second Adulthood. What may have been seen as a dead end is now perceptible as a gateway to years ahead that spread out like a brand-new playing field.

"I spent a large part of my early adult life on logistics— just getting from point A to point B with three young children and no money," said an animated fifty-nine-year-old schoolteacher, describing her postmenopausal change of outlook. "Now, with no responsibilities, with three functioning children who are off on their own, it's a liberation that is difficult to explain . . . it's emotional, physical, financial—total."

We have a second chance in postmenopause— unencumbered by the day-to-day caregiving and thousand and one details of feeling that most women pour into the long parental emergency—to focus on the thing we most love and to redirect our creativity in the most individual of ways. We must make an alliance with our changing bodies and negotiate with our vanity. No, we are never again going to be that girl of our idealized inner eye. The task now is to find a new future self in whom we can invest our trust and enthusiasm.

Today's "coalescents" are mapping out a whole new stage of life. Despite all the idiosyncrasies of this age group, common refrains emerged in the stories given by American women in their fifties:

"Making choices is so much easier" was a comment echoed from coast to coast.

"You don't get your period, and you don't have to panic when you don't," summed up a West Coast woman.

"You don't have to play the girl game anymore," said an attractive divorcée who's let her hair go gray. "But it's still all right to be a vulnerable female person and allow yourself moments of weakness. Now it's your choice."

The "empty nest" we were told by psychoanalytic theorists would leave us feeling useless and lacking in self-concept turns out not to register as a main concern in large-scale contemporary studies. When women mentioned it at all in interviews with me, it was usually with relief or relish.

"After being liberated from keeping those five long-legged sons filled up, a new world opened up to me as I approached fifty," said a southern woman who had happily fulfilled the duties of a full-time wife. "One of the kids said, 'Mom, what are you going to do with yourself now that we're all gone?' I said, 'Hon, I don't know, but count on it—I'm going to have fun!'"

"The freedom of middle age is fantastic!" exulted a former homemaker who loves her new life as a real estate maven. "Now Mom can lie down before dinner. Or I can pay somebody else to do dinner. Or I don't have to have dinner at all."

"Watch out, I'm heading downhill and I'm on a roll!" called a Colorado woman as she passed me on the jogging track.

A great discovery of the fifties is the *courage to go against*—against conformist behavior and conventional wisdom. A woman can at last integrate the rebellious boy in herself, left behind back when she was ten or eleven and eager for adventure and before she became vulnerable— i.e., capable of being impregnated. Social psychologist Bernice Neugarten reports that as women move into later life, they become more accepting of their own aggressive and egocentric impulses and feel less guilty. Research on female cognition has demonstrated that women shift more fluidly than men from intellect to intuition, or from linear to nonlinear thinking, seeing the events of life less as black and white than as a continuum.

Given the added status and confidence of the postmenopausal state, women are in an optimal position to voice their convictions and make a powerful public impact. An initial sense of timidity and danger may give way to relief and excitement, as the new older women realize there are still many "firsts" ahead. Once they stop clinging to a life and conditions that have been outgrown, they can stake out their freedom at last. This usually happens by the mid-fifties, as is evident in the following excerpts from interviews:

"I'm not pulling my punches like I used to—I'm saying more of the things I really think," boasted a beautiful Rochester woman, now sixty-eight, who has remade herself into an organizational management executive.

"I grew up mechanical, I could fix a flat or repair the roof, but I always deferred," admitted a well-built African-American woman of sixty who takes care of a three-family house. "Now I don't need anybody to tell me how."

"You have the whole spectrum of intellectual capacity to draw on," enthused a physician who left conventional medicine and is enlivened in her late fifties by practicing nutritional medicine.

Such comments hint at the welcome change of perspective as women come through the disequilibrium of menopause into the stage of mastery that follows it—a passage that is cause not for remorse but for celebration. In fact, my previous studies of life stages on sixty thousand adult

Americans established that women in their fifties, by self-report, had a greater sense of well-being than at any previous stage in their lives. A considerable body of psychological study data has accumulated since then confirming that women are least likely to be clinically depressed in middle age.

Extra-Sexual Passions

$\mathcal{A}$t a small conference on "The New Older Woman," organized by Group Four, a consulting partnership, and held at the Esalen Institute in summer 1991, prominent American women from diverse backgrounds and professions were invited to share viewpoints on what it's like to be energetic, ambitious, optimistic, and over fifty in today's America. Most said they had negotiated the passage through menopause with a minimum of difficulty. The happy little secret they shared was that they had enjoyed the best sex of their lives during and just after menopause, between the ages of forty-five and fifty-five. (Granted, their generation had been sexually repressed in youth.) These were also women of a generation totally unschooled in what to expect of menopause. The usual comment was that they were "too busy" with career, personal relationships, or family to dwell on the physical or psychological accompaniments to the Change of Life.

Participants now in their sixties or older agreed that there came a point, sometime in their fifties, when they had to let go—or at least stop trying to hang on to—their youthful image and move on. Although painful at the time, they had all found a source of new vitality and exhilaration—a "kicker." As each one described her personal struggle, a common denominator emerged and the group hit upon something profound:

The source of continuing aliveness was to find your passion and pursue it, with whole heart and single mind. It is essential to *claim the pause* and find this new source of aliveness and meaning that will make the years ahead even more precious than those past.

For several of the women the passion was to correct an ignored community or societal wrong: Harriet Woods, for example, the former lieutenant governor of Missouri, had lost a Senate race and turned to creating a brand-new political institution, a think tank at the University of Missouri. She went on to become president of the National Women's Political Caucus, the only bipartisan national membership organization that recruits, trains, and supports women for elective and appointive office. In both roles she pursues her passion: to help women learn to use power in ways different from hierarchical, victimizing male models, with an eye to transforming society. "Age no longer has the same relevance it used to have," she affirms. "Whether it is through caregiving or creating new institutions as I just did, it happens for women who are beyond what was once thought of as the curve for making a contribution."

Others had found more private passions: going back to school to finish a degree, writing a book, or pursuing knowledge in a special field for the pure pleasure of knowing.

It was agreed that the older woman with fewer resources often feels isolated, even cheated. Just as she feels free to pursue personal goals, her husband may be going into decline or physical dependency; returning children may try to manipulate her into remaining chief cook and laundry-woman; divorce or ailing parents may cramp her financially. But although these realities might sound like arguments against risk-taking at this time of life, in fact, they make it all the more essential to dare new explorations.

Vi Beaudry defied all these assumptions about the "trapped" menopausal woman, who is expected to feel too little self-worth to dare a divorce at such a precarious stage. Rather, her life started again in postmenopause, and it wasn't because she had an easy passage or plenty of money or fancy degrees. We met in a blue-collar redneck section of a southern city, the sort of place where, driving down Dixie Highway, Vi might stop for a light and suddenly have a Hooded Klansman in her face, thrusting literature through her window. When it happened, this steel magnolia pressed her 'gator boots to the gas pedal and just drove on. There is very little that makes her afraid anymore.

"It was my *husband* who had himself a menopause, okay?" she explains. He sat down in front of the TV and didn't get up for the next ten years. And it wasn't paid retirement. Vi was in her late forties when the siege began. She was the one having night sweats, but there was no time to indulge herself. Having done volunteer and unpaid political work while her children were still at home, Vi, as an overweight high school graduate, had to retool herself to enter the job market in a hurry. She tinted her hair strawberry blond, sewed herself a flattering wardrobe, and eventually moved out of clerking by creating a job for herself with the local cable company as its community services director.

"This time of menopause, just when you're expected to be falling down, you have to become self-supportive enough —economically, emotionally, spiritually—to go out on your own if you have to, and start another life," she has learned. On her fifty-seventh birthday, possessed of the postmenopausal courage to confront, Vi shook her husband out of his long day's TV doze.

"Today is my birthday," she announced. "My mother died when she was five years older than I am now. I do not want to live the rest of my life like this."

"What does your birthday have to do with it?" he said.

Okay, he didn't get it. She went into the kitchen and set down the clipboard that attested to her new authority as a member of the district sewer board. She looked at the rings flashing on her fingers and felt the gold lanyard looped around her semi-sheer blouse; she had bought them herself, all of it. It was quite a revelation: She did not need a man to live, and she wasn't living with a man. Vi went back and gave her husband an ultimatum. "I would like for you to contribute something to the running of the household by September first." When the date came and he demurred, Vi filed for divorce.

"I had a lot of readjustment to do," she admits. She had just paid off the mortgage on the house, but community property divorce laws forced her to mortgage it again. Vi needed a couple of years to rise above her anger. "But rather than be bitter about it, hey, you're buying back a life—not just holding on to a mortgage that would make you a prisoner for the rest of your life."

Neighbor women, still very southern in their ways, keep waiting for Vi to become depressed, feel socially invisible, go to seed. She laughs. "There are a lot of things worse than going home to an empty house." Hardly invisible, now sixty, she runs the community art festival, sits on several community boards, and is one of the most lusty, healthy, outspoken, self-confident people in town.

How—or if—one *welcomes* postmenopause, and consciously prepares for the new freedom it offers, makes all the difference in reaping the benefits of the stages beyond.

The gateway to our Second Adulthood is a passage to be approached with pleasurable anticipation, as we take control over our lives and assume the new license to be outrageous. Anthropologist Mary Catherine Bateson counsels: "Say to yourself, I'm going to start a new life. It could be a stage of expansiveness or withdrawal. It could be a time of introversion or of worldly adventure."

"Age rage," as psychologist Ellen McGrath describes it in her book on healthy depressions, is a predictable response to the downgrading that older women (and men) experience in most Western societies today. But a healthy depression is only transitional, until one moves through the passage and transforms old patterns of thinking and acting.

The key to finding a new sense of empowerment in the Second Adulthood comes from moving through the crisis of aging to *generativity*. This entails a profound shift, from pouring all one's energies into procreation or raising one's immediate children or into one's own advancement, toward feeling a voluntary obligation to care for others in a larger sense.

There is a natural generative role into which the postmenopausal woman comfortably fits, going back to prehistory. It is that of the matriarch. The historical biographer, Antonia Fraser, revels in this role. "People *love* women who have had lots of children," she purrs (she has had six). "When one says, 'I'm about to have my fourth grandchild and the fifth is on the way,' people say, 'Oh, isn't that wonderful? It makes them feel *tribally* good."

In preparing for a smooth postmenopausal passage, it is useful to look ahead to the most vital women of age and see how they have met the challenges of later-life passages. Cecelia Hurwich, one of the participants in the Esalen conference, had done a study over time on women in their seventies, eighties, and nineties for her doctorate at the

Center for Psychological Studies in Albany, California. The women selected had remained active and creative through unusually productive Second Adulthoods and well into old age. What were their secrets? we all wanted to know.

"They live very much in the present, but they always have plans for the future," Dr. Hurwich said. They had mastered the art of "letting go" of their egos gracefully so they could concentrate their attention on a few fine-tuned priorities. They continued to live in their own homes but involved themselves in community or worldly projects that they found of consuming interest. Close contact with nature was important to them, as was maintaining a multigenerational network of friends. And as they grew older they found themselves concerned more with feeding the soul than the ego.

Surprisingly, these zestful women were not in unusually good physical shape. They had their fair share of the diseases of age—arthritis, loss of hearing, impaired vision —but believing they still had living to do, they concentrated on what they could do rather than on what they had lost. Over the ten-year course of the study, most were widowed. This hardship, like so many others they had endured, they turned into a source of growth rather than defeat. Frequently they mentioned in conversation, "After my husband's death I learned to . . ."

Every one of them acknowledged the need for some form of physical intimacy; not, of course, just with a male. It might be with women friends, grandchildren, young people, but they found it was essential to have someone to touch, to hold, to share affection with. They found love through sharing the most natural of pleasures: music, gardening, hiking, traveling. Several spoke enthusiastically of having active and satisfying sex lives. One woman, asked how she felt about the automatic assumption that women in their seventies and eighties lost all interest in sex, answered after a long pause:

"This is how it is for me. I've become a vegetarian, but every once in a while I want a piece of red meat. And I go out and get it and eat it and enjoy it."

Wisewoman Power

Women who no longer belong to somebody now can belong to everybody—the community, a chosen circle of friends, a worship group, or even to the world—by virtue of contributing knowledge or creative insight or healing gifts. In fact, the elder women who survived in ancient or tribal cultures developed a way to further species survival *independent* of their wombs. These women became sources of experience and wisdom and were often venerated as shamans with healing powers, upon whom both individuals and tribe depended to handle crises. As the influence of female deities increased steadily up to about 500 B.C., the role of medicine man was assumed by medicine woman. "The fact that women were shamans during this period indicates they had entered into the most authoritative and honored ranks of healers," writes Jeanne Achterberg in *Woman as Healer*.

Wisdom, or the collective practical knowledge of the culture that is more simply termed common sense, has continued up through history to be associated with older women. Even in premodern times, when Christianity re-

,ected females as deities or primary healers, great public women did emerge and exert their influence though the religious system. Some became prized as advisers to emperors and popes, turned to for their healing powers, venerated as holy—and it turns out that they were usually near fifty when they took on this aura of wisewomen.

Today's pioneering women in postmenopause in advanced societies eventually give up the futile gallantry of trying to remain the same younger self. Coming through the passage of menopause, they reach a new plateau of contentment and self-acceptance, along with a broader view of the world that not only enriches one's individual personality but gives one a new perspective on life and humankind. Such women—there are more and more of them today—find a potent new burst of energy by their mid-fifties.

Margaret Mead spoke frequently about postmenopausal zest and regarded it as a widespread phenomenon. When Mary Catherine Bateson was writing her own book, *Composing a Life*, she was unable to find a formal discussion of the phenomenon mentioned by her mother. Yet Dr. Mead certainly experienced a grand bloom in her fifties, following on a shattering series of blows in her forties.

When the bomb exploded over Hiroshima, Mead tore up every page of a book she had nearly finished. As she wrote in her autobiography, *Blackberry Winter*, "Every sentence was out of date. We had entered a new age. My years as a collaborating wife also came to an end." She was forty-three. Her adored husband left the marriage, her closest colleague died, and she spent several years devising a new way of working without them, while improvising a life as a divorced professional mother of a small child.

But between the ages of forty-five and fifty-five, as Bateson pieces together the famous anthropologist's history, "she seemed to become prettier, she bought a couple of designer dresses for the first time, from Fabiani, and I think she started a new romantic relationship. Without question, she went through a complete professional renaissance." Boldly Dr. Mead decided to return to the field at the age of fifty-one. She boned up on languages she had learned twenty years before and went back to New Guinea, forging a major intellectual new start with groundbreaking research on social change published in the book *New Lives for Old*.

In fact, hormonal changes may partly explain why so many women describe a vastly increased store of energy after menopause, while some men move toward despair and decline. A good deal of the energy of a younger woman goes into producing enough of the hormone progesterone to sustain a possible pregnancy. Postmenopausal women no longer suffer from the handicap of continually fluctuating levels of progesterone. Menopause also puts an end to the mood swings of the menstrual years.

Middle-aged men have no such abrupt shutdown of hormone production and no accompanying surge of energy. "In my view, it's not so much that men decline, as that women start to overtake them," posits Dr. Katharina Dalton, a leading British endocrinologist. "It is also a medical fact that men's bodies age far faster than women's. Middle-aged men do not experience the new lease of life, the sense of liberation that postmenopausal women often enjoy. Their health gets worse, while that of their wives gets better."

This fact places many middle-aged wives in the role of woman-as-healer. They don't have to have the status of a prehistoric medicine woman or that of a medieval abbess to tap into their postmenopausal powers of active imagination, whereby they may be able to lead a seriously ill spouse or parent toward self-healing or spiritual comfort.

There is even a hormonal explanation to underscore the observation across cultures of the switch in male-female behavior during middle age, a phenomenon I've called the "Sexual Diamond." From their mid-forties to their sixties, women tend to become more aggressive and goal-oriented, while men show a tender and vulnerable side. As stated earlier, scientific studies show that after menopause, the ratio of male hormone (testosterone) to estrogen in a woman with ovaries shifts to about 20 to one. Dr. Howard Judd, the UCLA scientist who published the first study, acknowledges "this offers a potential hormonal explanation for the take-charge behavior so often exhibited by middle-aged women." Some experts estimate that this relatively high level of testosterone occurs in about 50 percent of postmenopausal females.

Meanwhile, men's testosterone levels are gradually decreasing with age, even as they continue to produce a relatively stable amount of estrogen. They may be going through their own version of "male menopause." A crisis of potency may be cued by relatively slight changes in sexual prowess. These changes are a combined product of the individual man's general health and hormone level, together with a psychological confrontation over what it means to be a man as his physical strength ebbs. Although men continue throughout the life cycle to produce 15 to 20 times more testosterone than women, what they begin to notice is the comparison with their own younger selves. Many men in their fifties shift to a lower gear, while their wives and female contemporaries often accelerate, fueled by their new postmenopausal energy and self-assertiveness.

"Do you know how you feel a week after your period ends—like you could climb mountains and slay dragons? That's how a postmenopausal woman feels all the time, if she's conscious of it," says Elizabeth Stevenson, a Jungian analyst in Cambridge.

Stevenson had a year of hot flashes, which she relieved with acupuncture, and by the age of fifty-two broke through to a state of postmenopausal zest. "It's both physical and psychological," she says. Now fifty-five, she doesn't have the same energy level she had at twenty-five, but she monitors and shepherds her energy so that her working days begin at eight and end at eight. If she eats right and exercises, she says, the consciousness of the wisewoman is always with her.

Emptying and Refilling

$\mathcal{M}$astering the physical and psychological challenges of the Change might be seen as a test, a necessary exercise, forcing us to look ahead and accept the new perspective coming into view. Each major life passage entails emptying and refilling. It is particularly literal, and poignant, during menopause. There is first the gushing, like the reddening of a tree as it blazes out in autumn with a flaming canopy before going dormant. As we move into postmenopause, we are emptied of the menses that has dominated our reproductive phase. We are reduced to basics, forced to lie fallow. Within that emptiness, watered by tears over the surrender of our magical powers of birthing, if we hold fast through the dark night of unknowing, we can discover our greater fertility. Contemplating the face of nature reminds us of our responsibility for creation and protection of the earth and of earth wisdom. While men are programmed by evolution to live short, high-performance lives, women are wired to endure.

The greatest boon of menopause is that it forces us to tune in to our body's needs and quirks and to stay intimately tuned. It is, after all, the house in which we will dwell for the rest of our days, and we will be comfortable in it only if we learn how to turn down the stress on our heart and keep the mineral turning over in our bone. A new balance must be struck between output and input. What is needed for replenishment? For some women it's the decision to take a four-day weekend every six weeks—to climb a mountain, look at the sea, or simply drop out with music or books—or whatever it takes to empty one's cares and find the calm for centering. For others, the Change is the signal to change unhealthy eating habits, stop smoking, invest in serious exercise, and learn what their body needs to feel good. For those who are already exercise habitués, they may need to balance aerobic exercise, which is demanding of the body, with yoga or meditation.

But more than that, of all the passages, the Change of Life is a process of emptying and refilling that requires a new companionship between mind and body.

I wasn't ready to be fifty until I was fifty-two. By then, I had made several logical steps up to a new perspective. If we allow the mind to expand and explore higher realities, the body follows. At some point over the course of those two years I suddenly knew, with utter certainty, that as I grew older I was going to get better. I invited my body to accept that new reality. I could begin to visualize, positively, the vast unmarked territory from here to my eighties. The journey excited me. I felt, almost giddily, like a pioneer. And by then, I had sorted out the practical aids and rituals that belonged in my long-term survival kit.

My personal choice, predicated on a family history of severe osteoporosis and no cancer, is to use hormone replacement therapy. It took me, however, a couple of years of experimentation before I found the right preparations and regimen to complement the peculiarities of my body chemistry. I am very glad I had the patience to stick it out.

Having systematically researched how to stem the crumbling, wherever I could, without surgery or making a fool of myself, I decided to let myself gain a little weight—it's called "sacrificing the fanny for the face." At the same time I am disciplined about daily exercise to keep my muscles tight, my bones strong, and my mental acuity pumped up with oxygen and those wonderful endorphins. Every woman is different, but for me, the daily ritual that keeps the motor purring is to down a dollop of Royal Jelly on awakening, to use nothing but natural oils on my face, and to take a jog on nice days or to work out with free weights and a treadmill. If time is short, I jump up and down on a tiny portable trampoline. I try to balance these weight-bearing efforts that are so good for the bones with meditation or a yoga class; it puts some elasticity back into sore sinews and stops the beat of urban life long enough to allow one to center.

Like many women who found motherhood deeply satisfying, I now find myself drawn irresistibly to gardening. Whether it's planting pots of petunias on a balcony or digging a fragrant herb garden, perhaps pitching earth and nurturing tender blooms is our subjective way of replacing the joy of growing babies. I plant a new tree each year and take pleasure in watching its progress like a child moving through school. And whenever I'm in London, I look for offbeat bulbs for my Shakespeare garden; they never fail to amaze and delight me when they finally sprout.

Vitamins are vital at this age—C, E, B-6, and of course calcium enriched with Vitamin D. Since natural sources of calcium are best, I take milk on my cereal and in my coffee, and often a glass of warm skimmed milk at night to put me to sleep. Annual mammograms and biannual bone-density checks are part of my discipline. Happily, I have *built* bone since I turned fifty with this regimen of exercise and hormone replacement. Finally, for husbanding my energy (and energizing my husband), I find that getting away together every six weeks or so for a long weekend adds immeasurably to the sweetness of life. And with our children grown, we can take off at the drop of a hat!

It has been a long road, but having "rounded the horn" I feel rekindled, high-spirited, and at home again inside my body. According to my husband, I look better, even younger, than I did when the journey began. (Thank goodness for the nearsightedness of middle age!) I am not the same me anymore. I am an older woman, that is true. The energy is not the same jumpy fits and starts sort I had as a younger woman; it is deeper, sustained, and with naps for refreshment, it seldom fails me. The outlines of my future self are coming into focus—and I like her. She is focused but not so driven. She dares me to follow my purest instincts in what I think and read and write, rather than what is expected or externally valued. Do serious work and try to make a difference in the world, yes, but she won't let me neglect that part of myself that wants to play, that is rediscovering the harmless things I did as a young girl—like getting lost in the woods. She dares me to take off on adventures. I've decided I'll go along on the trip with her, believing that the best stages are yet to be.

The magic charm, finally, is very simple. It is to say to yourself, *No, I won't go back. And I won't try to stay in the same place, inside the same skin. I will go forward. I will have the courage to take the next step.*

I believe it is vital to develop a future self in the mind's eye. She is our better nature, with bits and pieces of the most vital mature women we have known or read about and wish to emulate. If we are going to go gray, or white, we can pick out the most elegant white-haired woman we know and incorporate that element into our own inner picture. The more clearly we visualize our ideal future self, admire her indomitable skeleton and the grooves of experience that make up the map of her face, the more comfortable we will be with moving into her container.

An inspiring public model of wisewoman power is

Elizabeth Cady Stanton. As one who pursued justice for women well into her eighties, Stanton was living proof of her belief, which was eloquently recounted in her autobiography:

> The heyday of a woman's life is the shady side of fifty, when the vital forces heretofore expended in other ways are garnered in the brain, when their thoughts and sentiments flow out in broader channels, when philanthropy takes the place of family selfishness, and when from the depths of poverty and suffering the wail of humanity grows as pathetic to their ears as once was the cry of their own children.

Today's "coalescents"—both men and women—are mapping out a whole new stage of life for which evolution never provided. And we bring to it a broader view of the world. The source of continuing aliveness is to find your passion, and pursue it. It is essential to *claim the pause*. Remember, if forty-five is the old age of youth, fifty is the youth of a woman's Second Adulthood.

Postscript

$\mathscr{T}$o mark my own rite of passage through menopause I gave myself a few days alone in the mountains. I wanted to honor my graduation into the new stage of Second Adulthood and to reward my body for all the days it had already served me. On the last day I awoke after a full refreshment of sleep on a nearly empty stomach and opened the curtains to a dazzling sight.

The moon hung full over the hills. Unhurried by the day's first light, she reveled in her fullness. I went outside to sit in contemplation of her, and we faced each other in utter equanimity: She who had pulled the tides of my inner sea for 450-some months, powerfully, capriciously, violently, now had relaxed her hold on me and left my waters calm as a lagoon after a tropical storm. Emptied, I sat there in the twig-brushing breeze and savored the quiet aliveness that had come to me at last.

The moon began to sink, and I rose to fill my container with the new day. I felt pulled to hike once more up a mountain considered sacred by shamans who once ministered to the

Indians of this valley. Even then this mountain radiated a spiritual energy that drew those with the most subtle attunedness. Here the shamans marked rites of passage and performed rituals for birth and rites of fertility. It seemed an apt place to create my own ritual for marking this third blood mystery of a woman's life.

On the approach to the mountain my senses were quickened by each patch of herbs—the snap of sage, the tickle of thyme, the melancholy of rosemary, and what was that? The swoon of honeysuckle? Soon the scents were left behind as the bare rock and silver stubble of the foothills asserted their elemental simplicity. No frills here, only endurance. The wild herbs and grasses and desert flowers have the look of all healthily aging things: silvery gray, with strong roots, their flexible stems able to bend in the storm, their flowers calculated to bloom in the fissures between. All that is most creative and startling in life springs up in the cracks between.

As I followed the spiraling path up the mountain, lifting out of myself, I felt my inner world merging with the outer world. It was a world of silences, broken only by the munch of footfall on the crumbled earth and the sucking of Santa Ana winds. The moon was still in place. All at once the sun carved a dipper out of the opposite mountain and ladled its liquid gold down the face. The pure energy was almost overpowering. A sparkler of red and green spun for a few seconds in a mirrored circle beneath the great ball.

Then I sat for an undeciphered period of time in meditation on the brow of the far mountain. Honor the mellowed silence in you, I thought. Mark these moments when you are aware of not doing, not wanting, not preparing for the next activity, but simply filling with the moment. The more still I became, the more I was able to feel the earth traveling beneath me. I could see the sun hung over one horizon, ravishing, while behind me, in exactly the same position over the shadow side of the mountain, the moon was fading. The cymbals of day and night hung in perfect equipoise. The wind quieted.

Postscript

Then all at once I felt a surge of energy. Warm, whirling, giddy, it moved upward, setting words to buzzing in my brain. A sense of such exultation filled me. It was as if the hourglass had been turned over and the crystals of creative energy were flowing in reverse—from womb to mind. I couldn't wait to get back to my laptop, my writing . . . my passion.

We are all pilgrims together, finding our way, but the markers we lay along the trail will beckon future generations to even longer lives. Let us mark the way well. Filled with new life and license, let us bring the cymbals of light and shadow together and begin again.

Index